Blaze
of
GLORY

THE GLORY GARDENS SERIES
(in suggested reading order)

Blaze of GLORY

BOB CATTELL

Illustrations by
David Kearney

RED FOX

With thanks to Danial Khalid

A Red Fox Book

Published by Random House Children's Books
61-63 Uxbridge Road, London W5 5SA

A division of The Random House Group Ltd
London Melbourne Sydney Auckland
Johannesburg and agencies throughout the world

Text copyright © Bob Cattell 1997
Illustrations copyright © David Kearney 1997

Score sheets reproduced with kind permission of David Thomas
© Thomas Scorebooks 1985

First published in Great Britain by Red Fox 1997

This edition 2001

7 9 10 8

Set in Sabon by SX Composing, Rayleigh, Essex
Printed and bound in Great Britain by Bookmarque Ltd, Croydon, Surrey

THE RANDOM HOUSE GROUP Limited Reg. No. 954009

ISBN 978 0 099 72411 7

Contents

Chapter One

Marty raced in and bowled the first ball of the game. It was fast and short. A bouncer. The batsman leaned inside the line and hooked savagely.

We watched as the ball flew high off the top edge of the bat. It was going straight down Jacky's throat at long-leg. A wicket from the first ball, I thought; it was going to be a dream start to the tour. Jacky stood and waited just inside the boundary. The ball seemed to reach him more quickly than he expected. He tried to readjust as it hit his hands but it burst through his fingers and bounced over the rope for four. Marty groaned and sank to his knees in disappointment.

Jacky turned to pick up the ball; he bent down then he stopped and looked at his right hand. Immediately he turned and walked towards the pavilion. What was going on? We all watched him. "What's the matter, Jacky?" shouted Frankie. "It's a bit early for a drinks break."

Jacky didn't say a word. He held up his right hand towards us. The middle finger was sticking out backwards at right angles to the others. It looked disgusting.

"He's broken it," said Marty.

I couldn't believe it. After all the struggles to get Glory Gardens to Barbados: raising the money; persuading our parents; arranging the games – and now, after one ball of our first game, it looked as if Jacky's tour was already over.

Back row: Jacky, Marty, Clive, Cal, Mack, Matthew,
Front row: Ohbert, Azzie, Erica, Hooker, Frankie, Tylan, Jo

That's Jacky in the top left-hand corner of the picture – it was taken just before the game started. With Marty, Jacky makes up our opening bowling attack – so he's a really important member of the team. The other bowlers are Erica, me and the spinners, Cal and Tylan. I'm Hooker Knight, captain of Glory Gardens and the team's top all-rounder – although Erica and Cal are pretty useful at both batting and bowling, too.

The batting specialists are Matthew, who opens with Cal, and Glory Gardens' two class stroke-makers, Clive and Azzie. Frankie's our wicket-keeper, Mack's our star fielder and Ohbert is our specialist number 12 and all round special case. You'll see what I mean soon enough. Finally there's Jo, Frankie's sister, who is sitting on the right of the bottom row. She and Frankie don't just look different, they're complete opposites in absolutely every way. Jo's our scorer, team secretary and one of the main reasons we're here. She organises us, you see, and Glory Gardens takes an awful lot of organising.

But I'd better go right back to the very beginning.

Talk of a tour to Barbados started at the end of last season. At

8

first we thought it was a joke and hardly anyone took it seriously because under-13s teams just don't go on tours to Barbados . . . and anyway we didn't have any money. The people who were doing all the talking were Frankie and Clive.

Frankie's good at talking but, if you ask him to *do* anything, you've got to be a super-optimist to think it will happen. Clive's not exactly the most reliable person in the team, either. He's always late, especially for net practice. Clive's one of those really lucky people who are brilliant at sport without even trying but sometimes he forgets he's playing for a team instead of just for Clive da Costa. That's why he's not always very popular.

So, with Frankie and Clive in charge, none of the rest of us were getting too excited about Barbados. But, for once, they both persisted. Frankie wrote to Thompson Gale in Barbados. Thompson plays for Griffiths Hall, the top school team on the island – he's one of their demon fast bowlers. We came up against him and the Griffiths Hall team in our 'World Cup' tournament last summer. We just beat them in the final in one of the greatest games of cricket ever played.

Last season was brilliant for Glory Gardens. First we won the North and East County Under-13s League. Then we clinched the 'World Cup' against loads of 'international' teams. And, finally, right at the end of the season we went to Edgbaston and triumphed in the national Champions League competition over top opposition from all round the country.

You should have seen the local paper that week. The headline was "*Glory Gardens – National Champs*" and there was a whole page about our famous victory. It began: "*Two years ago Glory Gardens Cricket Club didn't even exist. Then a group of young cricketers decided it was time to form their own club. They named it after Glory Gardens recreation ground where they'd first played together. And now, two years on, they are champions of England.*"

It was on the television news, too. And everyone was talking about our great Edgbaston victory. Maybe we had been a bit lucky to win on the day. It was hard to believe that we were the best under-13 team in the country – no team with Ohbert in it

9

could be that good. But we've improved fast and there's not a side anywhere keener than Glory Gardens.

I think our fame helped us to get to Barbados – because suddenly things started to happen. Frankie got a letter from Thompson Gale saying that his school would fix all the games for us with the best teams on the island. He made it sound dead easy – and he also told Frankie to prepare for the biggest thrashing of our lives.

"Thommo's got a short memory," said Frankie. I'd better send him the score-sheet for the World Cup final to remind him how good we are."

It was about then that Clive's aunt started to take an interest in things. She was born in Barbados, and she's mad about cricket. Clive has lived with her ever since his old man left home and just disappeared. Clive hasn't seen him from that day which is partly a good thing because his father was a terrible drunk and sometimes used to beat him up. Clive's improved a lot since then – he's still arrogant but nowhere near as bad as he was.

Without saying a word to any of us Clive's aunt applied to the Lottery for funding for our trip. The first we knew of it was when Frankie rushed into school one morning with the news that we'd got the money.

"They'll pay half the cost of the tour if we can raise the other half," he said. "Clive rang to tell me. It's amazing isn't it?"

"What's amazing is your imagination," said Tylan – to be honest we all thought it was one of Frankie's wind-ups.

"Wicket-keeper's honour," protested Frankie. "Would I lie to you about something like this?"

"You'd lie about anything, fatman," said Cal. So how much money have we still got to find?"

"A lot," said Frankie, calming down slightly. "But we can do it. We've got months before the tour."

It was only when Kiddo turned up to confirm Frankie's story that we finally believed him. Kiddo Johnstone is our coach. He opens the batting for Eastgate Priory Firsts and ages ago – before he got this knee injury – he used to play county cricket. Kiddo helped us get Glory Gardens started and the truth is that we owe him a lot. There's only one serious thing wrong with Kiddo – he's our French teacher. Still it's not hard to see that he prefers teaching cricket to French any day and he was almost as excited as Frankie about the Lottery money.

"I'm beginning to think, kiddoes, that the gods are smiling on us. We might just have us a tour." Kiddo talks like that all the time. He never uses one word when he can find six and arrange them in a weird order. "Mind you," he went on, "it's going to be mighty hard work raising the money. You're all going to have to put your shoulders to the wheel and heave."

Frankie volunteered to take charge of fund-raising but Jo wasn't having that. "You're having nothing to do with money while I'm secretary of Glory Gardens," she said to her older brother.

"Sorry, Frankie," said Cal. "You've done really well so far but you know she's right."

Frankie looked a bit dismal but he never argues with Jo. No-one does.

"That's agreed then," said Jo. "I'll organise it."

So the serious fund-raising started. Matthew who is the club treasurer kept a daily record of the money as it came in. At the end of one month he had a list like this:

Existing club funds		£77.50
Knicker rota		£88.27
Sponsored indoor cricket tournament		£218.00
Glory Gardens raffle (so far)		£43.20
Car boot sale		£69.44
Frankie's duck race		£1.40
Donations:	Ian Botham	£50.00
	Eastgate Priory C.C.	£50.00
	County Cricket Club	£100.00
	Others	£28.42
Total		£726.23

I could believe we'd raised so much money. Azzie's dad ran the indoor cricket tournament and it was a brilliant success. The team he selected beat us in the semi-finals and went on to win the competition. He was really delighted about that and, I suppose, he deserved it. After all we had thrashed his team in the 'World Cup'. The car boot sale was organised at the Priory by Clive's aunt and Kiddo was in charge of the raffle.

The knicker rota is our regular money earner for the club. Each of us is supposed to take turns working on Tylan's dad's market stall every Saturday morning – but in fact Ohbert does it far more than anyone else because he really enjoys it and he earns twice as much money as the rest of us. The stall sells mostly underwear, which is why we call it the knicker rota, and our money comes from tips and the odd fiver from Ty's old man if he's had a good day and he's feeling generous. It was Ohbert who had the idea of putting up a notice saying: *Donate your spare change to Glory Gardens' tour of Barbados*. Some miserable people said why should kids like us go on holiday abroad when they themselves couldn't even afford a holiday in England, but loads of them gave us money, especially the stall owners.

The only complete fund-raising disaster was Frankie's duck race. Holding a duck race in the middle of winter didn't seem a good idea in the first place. Then Frankie forgot to tell anyone it was taking place till the last moment so hardly anyone turned up – which, as things turned out, was probably a good thing.

It rained for two whole days before the race. We assembled along the muddy banks of the Mill Brook on a cold Saturday afternoon. I'd never seen the stream so full, the water was racing along like a mountain torrent. Frankie lined up the little plastic ducks he'd borrowed from the Priory club along the bank and we all chose a duck for a £1.

"The winner gets a bottle of whisky," said Frankie gathering up his ducks for the start of the race. The whisky had been donated by Azzie's dad. When Frankie finally let the ducks go they took off so fast downstream that we couldn't keep up with them. At least half of them were washed over the net at the end of the race and bobbed merrily off towards the sea, lost forever. Frankie panicked and tried to catch them. With one hand clutching the branch of a tree he swung precariously out over the rapids and . . .

"Watch out, Frankie," yelled Marty. "That branch doesn't look . . ." SPLASH. ". . . too safe." Cal finished the sentence and peered down at Frankie who was struggling and gurgling in the freezing waters. He was muddy, smelly and shivering when Marty, Cal and I finally pulled him out. And all he got for his efforts was a terrible cold because he had to spend most of his 'winnings' on buying a new set of plastic ducks.

But it was Frankie who got £50 out of Ian Botham. He wrote to him and asked if he'd appear in a pantomime which Frankie himself was going to write and act in. It was one of his daftest ideas but Ian Botham wrote back very politely to say that he was very sorry that he was busy but he wished us luck, said we'd have a wonderful time in Barbados and sent a cheque for £50. Frankie showed it to everyone at school before handing it over to Matthew.

Successful though our fund-raising had been, however, it was still nowhere near enough. If we didn't come up with a big idea very soon there'd be no Lottery money and no tour.

As usual Marty was the most pessimistic. "It's hopeless. We might just as well give the money back and forget all about Barbados."

"But we don't know who gave us most of it," said Matthew.

"Then we can blow it on an enormous feast," said Frankie. We've got enough to eat for a week like the Romans did." We were all completely stumped for ideas for raising the extra cash – except, of course, Frankie. He had plenty of suggestions such as kidnapping Ohbert and holding him up for ransom or charging an entrance fee for maths lessons or busking in the high street. The Frankie Allen One-Man Band was nearly arrested outside the town hall after only one song.

In the end the breakthrough came from the most unlikely person.

Chapter Two

"**W**hy are you so miserable?" asked my sister one morning.

"What's it to do with you," I said.
"I bet I can guess what it's about."
"What?"
"Stupid cricket."

As you may have guessed I don't normally talk to Lizzie much. First because she's so irritating. And secondly because usually all I want to do is clonk her over her head for being my sister. I've made a vow never to talk to her about cricket because that just gives her the chance to make fun of me and she doesn't need more than one invitation to do that. She may be only little but she knows exactly how to get on my nerves.

Lizzie has a sort of love-hate relationship with Glory Gardens. She's always telling me how boring cricket is, but on the other hand it was she who made our mascot for us. It's a sort of soft, squidgy thing which looks like it's made out of old socks. It's supposed to be modelled on Kiddo's dog, Gatting, but it doesn't look a bit like him. All its stuffing is coming out now and Lizzie complains that we don't look after it properly which is true because we usually throw it round the changing room after matches. The only reason we hang on to it is because Jo thinks it brings us luck and she likes to have it sitting on the table in front of her when she's scoring.

It turned out that Lizzie knew everything about the Barbados tour and the trouble we were having raising money. I don't know who told her. Not me, that's for sure.

"It will be a pity if you don't go," she said. 'I was looking forward to getting rid of you for a few days."

"Then all you've got to do is find someone to give us the rest of the money," I said. How much have you got in your piggy bank?"

Lizzie thought for a moment. "What about getting a sponsor?"

"What?"

"You know, a sponsor. People who put their names on your shirts and . . . your bats and caps too, I suppose."

"I know what a sponsor is," I said crossly. "But who would want to sponsor us? We're not famous or on the telly."

"But you're quite well known round here since your silly final at Edgbaston," she said. "Anyway I was only trying to help." She looked rather cross that I wasn't impressed with her great idea and to cheer her up I said maybe she was right and I'd talk to the others about it.

I didn't give it another thought until I was buying a cricket shirt at Ollie's Sports Shop in Baxter Street and the sponsor's logo caught my eye. Why not ask Ollie about it, I thought. I told him about the tour and the Lottery money and he got more and more interested. Then I mentioned Lizzie's sponsorship idea. "I think I might be able to help you there," said Ollie.

A week later Glory Gardens' tour of Barbados had not one but two sponsors – Ollie's Sports Shop and Gunn & Moore, the cricket bat makers. They gave us shirts and caps with their names printed on them, some really good new cricket bats and a kit bag. Finally there was the cheque; it was a big one and it meant our fund-raising worries were nearly over.

Lizzie was unbearable when she found out about it. "See, I said it was a great idea," she gloated.

"Yeah, thanks," I said.

"Don't you think you owe something, then?"

"Such as?"

"Well," said Lizzie thinking hard. "The least you can do is promise to send me a postcard every day from Barbados."

I moaned a bit but in the end I said I would – on my honour. And then six weeks later we were in Barbados playing our first game

15

against Carlton School.

But already it was all going wrong. After one ball of our first game we were down to ten players. With Jacky injured there was nothing for it but to send for our twelfth man. Ohbert didn't waste any time changing; he came on to the pitch dressed as he was – in lime green shorts and a coloured tee-shirt that would have made a Premier League goalkeeper jealous.

He ambled on and I shouted and tried to direct him to long-leg but he took no notice and walked all the way to the middle of the pitch. I could just imagine what the Carlton players were thinking at the sight of this odd, skinny apparition. And when they saw him play it would be even worse.

"Oh but . . . Hooker, where do you want me to field?" asked Ohbert eventually.

"Long-leg," I said, trying to keep calm.

"That's back where you came from and turn left," said Cal.

Ohbert set off towards long-off. "The other way, Ohbert," shouted Frankie.

Ohbert walked past me again, "Oh, but . . . Hooker. You should see Jacky's finger. It's like this." Ohbert bent his middle finger back as far as it would go until he winced with pain. "Only worse." He grinned stupidly and disappeared roughly in the direction of long-leg and I prayed that there wouldn't be another top-edged hook. But I knew from experience that the harder I tried to hide Ohbert in the field the more the ball would be drawn to him.

At last, after a break of at least ten minutes, Marty bowled the second ball of his opening over. It was short again and once more the opener hooked; this time it flew off the middle of the bat and bounced just once before flying across the rope. Ohbert raced to retrieve it.

Welcome to Caribbean cricket, I thought and I went over and had a quiet word with Marty.

"I've never seen luck like it," complained Marty.

"If you keep pitching short he'll stay lucky," I said. "Bowl it up. Make him play you off the front foot."

Marty grunted and snatched the ball angrily. He strode back to his mark. But the next ball was a good, block-hole yorker and the batter only just dug it out in time. Even so, at the end of the over Carlton had 11 on the board. I decided a change of tempo was needed. They seemed to be pretty good against quick bowling, so how would they get on against some really slow stuff? I brought Cal on to bowl his off-breaks from the other end.

"I don't think they're going to play me defensively," said Cal. "What about a few fielders out on the boundary." I gave him a deep extra-cover and a deep mid-wicket. But I kept the rest of the field in the ring. If Carlton were going to hit Cal they'd have to go over the top.

Cal's first ball was driven hard to Mack in the covers and he stopped it with a brilliant sliding dive. He didn't look very pleased

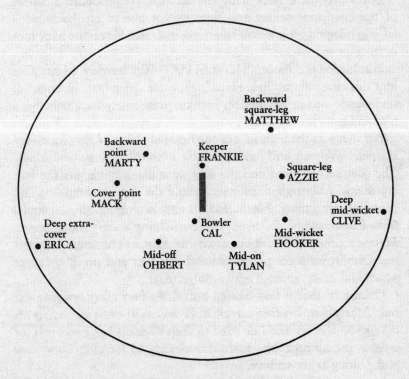

Cal bowls to a field with five on the leg side

when he got to his feet – the ground was as hard as concrete and it was like diving on the school playground. Mack inspected a bruised and grazed arm and elbow and a tear in the knee of his trousers.

Cal got the hang of the wicket very quickly. It was so hard and fast that he realised he had to bowl a touch short of his usual length to avoid being driven. But he mixed it up with a good slower ball and a quicker one at yorker length fired into the leg stump.

"Okay, so far," he said to me at the end of his first over. But there's no turn there."

"Do you think Tylan will get any spin?" I asked.

"He usually does," said Cal. Tylan bowls wrist spin and he's a big turner of the ball on most surfaces. If Marty couldn't find his rhythm I was tempted to go for an all spin attack.

But Marty came back with a vengeance. He produced a couple of toe crushing yorkers and then he got one to nip back off a length; it kept a bit low, too and the opener was hit on the back foot in front of the wicket.

Frankie led the shout. "HOWZTHAT! Well bowled, Marty. Got him this time. Plumb lbw. Hard luck, mate. Nice little innings." If the umpire was in any doubt, Frankie must surely have convinced him and up went the finger.

But that was the highlight of the first half-hour of play for Glory Gardens. We were still having trouble with the strange conditions. The ground was hard and the ball went like a bullet off the bat. Frankie was having a nightmare behind the stumps, fumbling and dropping everything. He fluffed an easy stumping off Cal and I soon lost count of the byes. The outfielding wasn't much better. Matthew dropped a hard but catchable chance at backward square-leg. Ohbert let a couple go through his legs and no-one, except Mack and Erica, seemed really motivated.

On top of that it was baking hot. After four overs bowling flat out, Marty was looking wrecked. It was a 30-overs game, so his maximum was six and I decided to keep back his last two overs for later in the innings. The score was already 43 for one. They were going along at six an over.

It was time for Erica to take over at the top end. As always she immediately found an immaculate length. It said a lot for her accuracy that though the batsmen were looking for runs they couldn't get her away even on this fast track. She and Cal bowled in tandem for five overs and we got some sort of control back. But when Cal came to the end of his spell we had still only taken the solitary wicket.

As usual everyone was full of advice about who should bowl next.

"Why don't you have a go?" said Frankie to me. "We might as well get the rubbish out of the way as soon as we can."

"I have a better idea," said Cal. "Give Frankie an over or two. At least he won't be able to let all those byes through if he's bowling."

Mack was swinging his arm over and Clive was jumping up and down and pointing to himself. He always thinks he ought to bowl – and I usually ignore him. It's not that he's no good but I prefer to stick to the regulars unless something goes seriously wrong and I need a change bowler. I decided it was time for Tylan and his leggies.

"I'm going to give you six on the off-side – so you'd better bowl straight," I said to Ty.

Tylan grinned. "Outrageous. Don't I always?"

There was plenty of bounce in the pitch for him and he certainly managed to get the ball to turn. But it was his first long hop that took the wicket. The opening bat slammed it straight at Mack who was standing in acres of space at mid-wicket; he was the only close fielder on the leg sideand he took the catch comfortably. After 14 overs they were 63 for two.

But, as the batsmen got used to him, Tylan's loose balls started to prove expensive. It was a pity, because Erica was bowling really tightly at the other end and the more we kept up the pressure the more likely they were to make mistakes. Already we were missing Jacky in a big way.

After three overs of Tylan's spin I decided it was time for me to take over from him at the bottom end. Before I did Erica got a well deserved wicket – a thin snick to Frankie and for the first time in the innings he did something right and held on to a good, low, one-handed catch. He celebrated with a great howl and ran round the field delivering high fives to everyone in sight. He nearly knocked Ohbert off his feet.

"Calm down, fatman. You'll have a heart attack," said Cal as Frankie zoomed past him on his second circuit.

If the ball is coming through reasonably high the keeper can take it with both hands but here the ball is low and dropping and Frankie takes it in his right glove. When you dive take your head towards the ball. This helps you to keep your eyes on it and it gets your body in the right place.

"What a catch. I wish I could see a replay," enthused Frankie.

I began my spell against the new batsman. I like that because you always feel you're in with a chance when someone new comes to the crease. The main thing was to make him play at every ball and not give him any sighters. I missed my run up on my first ball and bowled a no-ball.

I began to see why Marty was having trouble bowling on this pitch. It was slightly raised which meant that you had to come uphill in the final stride or two. And it was lightning quick – so anything overpitched disappeared through the covers or past mid-off for four. That's just what happened to my third delivery. Then I beat the outside edge of the bat a couple of times and began to feel a little better.

Erica had now finished her spell – she'd taken one for 17. I brought back Marty at the top end to replace her. With his third ball he had the new batsman playing all round a well-disguised slower ball and it hit the top of the middle stump. In came the next Carlton player who immediately pulled Marty for four, bringing up the hundred.

In my next over I felt that at last I was getting the hang of bowling on this pitch. My biggest worry now was Frankie. He dropped another catch off Marty and the number of byes he'd let through was now well into double figures. Every time he fumbled the ball there was a big sigh from the Glory Gardens' players – especially Marty and Clive.

I went over and had a word with him but before I could speak he said, I know, that's 13 byes. I'm not doing it on purpose, you know." By Frankie's standards he was sounding quite worried.

"Maybe you're standing too far up for the quickies."

"But then I'll miss the catches."

"You usually drop them anyway," I said unkindly.

Frankie looked at me and then he grinned. "Don't worry, Skip. It'll be okay from now on, I promise." Next ball he let through another bye off my bowling.

There were now six overs left. With Marty bowled out I needed someone to deliver the remaining three from the top end. I was worried that Tylan would be too expensive and I went for Mack. It was my biggest mistake of the day. We took ages between us to place the field and it was a complete waste of time. Mack bowled a dreadful over and it was carved for 12 runs by their classy number three bat, Everton Payne.

"Thanks, Mack," said Frankie as Mack walked slowly back to his fielding position at extra-cover. "We'll let you know."

Mack scowled. Even he wasn't his usual bouncy, talkative self today.

The fourth ball of my next over was dispatched back over my

21

head for four by Everton. I looked at the score-board and 49 went up against his name. Right, I thought, you're not scoring your fifty off me. I had him tucked up with an in-cutter and then I bowled one just short of a length outside the off-stump. Everton went for a screaming drive on one knee and the ball flew low and hard into the covers. It was well to Mack's left but he took off and caught it inches from the ground with both hands. It was a spectacular catch and Everton, though he must have been disappointed as hell to miss his fifty, gave Mack a little nod of approval before he walked off.

"He can't bowl, but can he catch," shouted Frankie.

Mack inspected another set of grazes on his arm and then looked up at Frankie. "I can keep wicket, too, if you'd like to come and dive about on this concrete instead."

"Thanks, Mack. You can take a rest from bowling now," I said.

"There's gratitude for you," said Mack with a grin.

With Everton gone I now felt I could bring Tylan back and I felt completely justified when, with his third ball, he took a wicket. The batsman came down the pitch to him and Frankie's stumping was only the second good thing he'd done all day. It didn't, of course, stop him from doing another lap of honour.

Quite suddenly I was bowling the last over of the innings. The field was set well back and there were plenty of singles to be taken. But the batsmen weren't looking for singles. With 144 on the board, they were after boundaries. I bowled two yorkers – the second was worth a big shout for lbw but it went for leg-byes instead. Then the batsman played and missed and gave Frankie a chance to add to his record total of byes. A wild swing on the leg side fell clear of the field and there were two easy runs but the batters decided to take on Cal's throw and go for the third. The ball fizzed in low and straight to me at the bowler's end and I had the bails off long before the batsman slid his bat in.

The 150 came up next ball – fittingly another bye to Frankie. And so I bowled the last delivery of the innings. It was swung away off a good length high in the air to the mid-wicket boundary. Cal and Ohbert both converged on it. "It's Cal's," I shouted. "Stop Ohbert. Stop." Cal shouted too – but Ohbert kept running. As Cal steadied himself to take the catch I saw what was going to happen and I shut my eyes.

"Look out, Cal," screamed Azzie.

Cal stood his ground. He pouched the ball in both hands and then ducked as he caught sight of Ohbert flying towards him. Ohbert bounced off Cal's back, took off, flew over Cal's head, hovered in the air for a split second and landed upside down in a blur of colour, right in front of the pavilion. As Ohbert picked himself up Cal held up the ball and received a round of applause from the small crowd in the pavilion. Ohbert stood up and looked puzzled and then he bowed to the crowd. The applause immediately turned to laughter.

"Oh but . . . I bet he didn't feel a thing," said Frankie.

"Of course he didn't, he landed on his head," said Tylan.

We walked towards the pavilion and Kiddo came out to meet us. He went straight for Frankie. "Oh no, he's going to lecture me about all those byes," said Frankie.

"Frankie Allen," shouted Kiddo, "What do you think you look like?"

"Look like? Sorry, Mr Johnstone, me?"

"Those socks. You don't wear red socks on a cricket pitch. And you certainly don't tuck your trousers into them."

Frankie sighed and looked down at his feet. Then he looked at Ohbert in his shorts and amazing shirt. "Why pick on me?" he muttered.

| INNINGS OF CARLTON SCHOOL | TOSS WON BY CARL. | WEATHER HOT |

	BATSMAN	RUNS SCORED	HOW OUT	BOWLER	SCORE
1	M. ALLEYNE	4.4.1.1.2	lbw	LEAR	12
2	J. CLARKE	2.1.2.1.2.2.1.1.1.2.1.2	ct McCURDY	VELLACOTT	18
3	E. PAYNE	4.2.2.2.2.1.2.2.1.1.1.2.2.2. 2.2.1.2(35).2.4.4.4	ct McCURDY	KNIGHT	49
4	B. WILLIAMS	4.1.3.4.2.1.2	ct ALLEN	DAVIES	17
5	C. HILLABY	1.4.1	bowled	LEAR	6
6	S. BENTHAM	4.2.3.2.3	NOT OUT		14
7	G. BABBS		st ALLEN	VELLACOTT	0
8	O. CHANCE	2.1.2.2	Run OUT		7
9	M. MULLINS		ct SEBASTIEN	KNIGHT	0
10	T. SEARLE				
11	B. WILDEY				

FALL OF WICKETS

	1	2	3	4	5	6	7	8	9	10
SCORE	17	63	90	97	131	134	149	150		
BAT NO	1	2	4	5	3	7	8	9		

BYES 2.1.1.1.1.1.1.1.2.1.2 1.1	16	TOTAL EXTRAS 27
L.BYES 1.1.1.2.1.1.2	9	TOTAL FOR WKTS 150
WIDES		
NO BALLS 1	1	

SCORE AT A GLANCE

BOWLING ANALYSIS · NO BALL + WIDE

	BOWLER	1	2	3	4	5	6	7	8	9	10	11	12	13	OVS	MDS	RUNS	WKT
1	M. LEAR	4+.1.2	.2	22.2	2.2.2	X	..W.4.	1.2							6	0	30	2
2	C. SEBASTIEN	..1.1	.21.4.	.1.2	.1.2	4...2.	..1.2.	X							6	0	21	0
3	E. DAVIES	1.1	.2.	.1.1	.2..2.3.	.1..W.1	X								6	0	17	1
4	T. VELLACOTT	.1.2W.	.4.2.21	.2.21	X	3.W.1.2	3.2								5	0	29	2
5	H. KNIGHT	9.4.1	.2	M	4.W	.2.1.W									6	1	16	2
6	T. McCURDY	2.4.4.2	X												1	0	12	0
7																		
8																		
9																		

Chapter Three

Back in the pavilion we all crowded around Jacky to get a look at his finger. It was dislocated, not broken, and luckily one of the Carlton supporters was a doctor.

"She just gave it a big pull and, click, it went back in its socket," said Jacky. "It didn't half hurt though."

Tylan groaned and held his stomach. The finger had already swelled up to twice its normal size and it was turning blue and purple and yellow.

"I've got to go and have it X-rayed," said Jacky. Just to check the bone's not chipped."

"How long before you can play again?" I asked.

"It depends. The doc said I'd be lucky to bowl on this tour. But I had a bet with her that I will." Jacky was obviously really disappointed but he was putting a brave face on it. He'd had a terrible time with injuries lately – he missed out on the final at Edgbaston at the end of last season, too.

Kiddo had a word with us all before we went into bat. If I know anything about West Indian cricket, kiddoes, they'll have a few quickies and they'll probably let you have it short and fast for the first few overs. Don't worry though. Get your heads down, your eyes in and don't worry about the runs. They'll come soon enough on this track. Just lean into the ball and it's four runs."

"I've never seen such a hard wicket," I said looking towards the strip which was shining in the sun.

"They soak it with water," said Kiddo. "And then, when it has dried a bit, they roll it hard. You can see, there's virtually no grass and it's polished on the top. They do that with a roller – twisting it from side to side until the pitch comes up like glass. It makes it fast with lots of bounce."

"Remember, Cal, eyes down and head off," said Frankie slapping Cal on the back. "And best of luck."

Cal was opening the innings as usual with Matthew who hadn't yet appeared from the changing room. This was my full batting order:

Matthew Rose
Cal Sebastien
Azzie Nazar
Clive da Costa
Erica Davies
Hooker Knight
Mack McCurdy
Frankie Allen
Tylan Vellacott
Marty Lear
Ohbert Bennett

Ohbert shouldn't really have been in the batting line-up because he'd only fielded as a sub. But their captain, Bryan Williams said Ohbert could bat because he had fielded for the whole innings except one ball. It was a nice gesture – particularly since he didn't know that Ohbert's batting was worse than useless.

At last Matthew emerged from the changing room. He was wearing two thigh pads, an arm protector and a white helmet.

"You've forgotten your breast plate and your shield, Matt," said Frankie, bouncing the cricket ball off his helmet.

"I don't care what anyone thinks, I'm wearing it," said Matthew.

"Quite right, kiddo," said Kiddo. "If it makes you feel more comfortable you use it. I didn't wear a helmet in my time in first-class cricket. Hardly anyone did. But today I'd wear one like a flash. If you don't it's like saying 'I'm too good for a helmet' and then the quickies will really work you over. Whether you need one at your "age or not – only you can decide."

"Where'd you get it from?" asked Mack.

"My mum gave it to me for Christmas. She bought it from Ollie's."

"Oh but, can I borrow it when I bat, Matthew?" asked Ohbert. He'd even taken his Walkman off to admire Matthew's headgear.

Frankie laughed. "It would be impossible to damage your brain, Ohbert."

"If it fits you you can wear it, Ohbert," said Matthew. "That's assuming, of course, I'm out when you come in." And he smiled and went out to bat.

Kiddo was right about the bowling; it was quick, short and lethal. Bryan Williams came down the hill and bowled six short-pitched deliveries which had Matthew swaying and ducking and probably made him feel very pleased he was wearing his Christmas present.

The bowler at the other end was a left-armer who came over the wicket and got the ball to lift and move away outside the off-stump. Cal edged one for four and then tickled another straight into first slip's safe hands. 4 for one.

Azzie announced his arrival at the wicket by driving his first ball on the up for four. Matthew followed that by blocking out another maiden over at the other end – although he took two leg-byes when he ducked into a bouncer and it went off his shoulder past the keeper.

Azzie and Matthew seemed, at last, to be getting used to the pace of the pitch and the runs were starting to flow steadily when Azzie got a short one down the leg side and went for the hook. He must have just touched it as it flashed past and the keeper and all the close fielders went up in a concerted appeal. Azzie walked without looking at the umpire. We were 21 for two.

Clive looked more determined than I've ever seen him going out to bat. It was his first innings in Barbados and his aunt was watching him. This tour meant a lot to Clive; it was as if he had something to prove to himself.

Most of the time on the cricket field Clive gives the impression that he's hardly awake. Batting and fielding come so easily to him and he just ghosts through a game – doing everything better than most of us without any real effort. Today was different. There was a steely expression on his face as if he really meant business and his first scoring short – a controlled straight drive – looked gritty rather than the loose, flowing style we've all come to expect from Clive.

It wasn't long before he overtook Matthew. Then he hit a blistering four off Bryan Williams – it went to the right of cover point and the fielder didn't even move.

The opening bowlers both came to the end of their spells and were replaced by two more quickies who were every bit as fast. In fact one of them, who bowled right-arm round to both Matthew and the left-handed Clive, was probably the quickest of the lot.

"He's running on the pitch," complained Erica, after we'd watched a couple of balls from the new bowler. It was true – his run-up brought him in at an angle and his right boot dragged across the wicket in front of the off-stump before he veered away on the follow-through.

"If he carries on like that it'll be a dream for an off spinner," said Cal.

"I think he's doing it deliberately," said Marty.

Clive noticed it too, and we saw him point the foot marks out to the umpire. Off the very next ball Clive brought up our fifty with a lovely back-foot drive. But it wasn't just Clive who was playing well. Matthew was doing more than just hold up an end. He hit two lovely off drives followed by a delicate leg glance.

"Are you sure that's Matthew out there?" said Frankie. "I'm beginning to think it's someone else wearing his helmet."

At the end of 18 overs we were on 68 for two and going well. Clive had 29 and Matthew 13. The right-arm round bowler had twice been warned for running on the pitch by the umpire but as far as we could see he was still doing it.

Then there was another change of bowling. A small lad with glasses started warming up. He tossed a couple of balls at one of the fielders.

Matthew starts his innings by building up his confidence and playing most of his shots in the 'V' between mid-on and mid-off with a completely straight bat. This drive off the back foot ends with a check finish. The ball is played between mid-off and the bowler. Look how Matthew follows the ball right to the end of the follow-through.

"What did I tell you," said Marty. An offie. And he's coming on at the top end to bowl into those foot marks."

For once Marty's prediction was right – even the worst of pessimists has to get it right once in a while. The spinner's first ball was a full toss and Clive smacked it away on the leg side for four. The next one was on a length and it turned and shot along the ground. Clive was late on it and over went his middle stump.

"Well bowled, Gus," shouted the keeper. Lovely ball."

"If he keeps hitting that rough we're dead," said Marty.

"Give it a break, Mart," said Cal. "He's only a spinner, after all.

I thought you told me all spinners were rubbish."

Erica joined Matthew and nothing unusual happened for the rest of the spinner's over. The quickie continued from the other end and he was again warned for running on the pitch.

Next over the spinner found the spot again with his second ball. It took off. Erica snatched her bat away but the ball just flicked her gloves on the way through to the keeper. I jumped up from my seat because I was in next.

I took guard very carefully and then inspected the worn patch just outside the off-stump. If I got down the wicket to the ball I reckoned I could play it on the full before it pitched in the rough. I waited as the spinner ran in and bowled and I went down the pitch to the first ball I received. As I played it I knew I'd misread the length. I missed and heard the dreadful click of the ball hitting the stumps then a huge cheer. I'd gone for a golden duck.

Next over Mack was caught at mid-wicket and we'd slumped hopelessly from 72 for two to 80 for six.

"Play straight. No wild swings," I told Frankie.

"That spinner was born to be whacked," said Frankie ominously.

"Francis. You're not listening. How are you going to bat?" asked Jo sternly.

"Straight, I promise," said Frankie and he strolled off to the middle.

And for an over or two he remembered his promise. But then he must have looked up at the score-board and realised that we had only 88 runs and there were just six overs left. He drove the spinner straight back over his head for four and, encouraged by that, carted the very next ball wild and high straight into the hands of the deep square-leg.

"Sorry," he said, head down, as he walked towards us. "Sometimes I hear noises in my head which tell me to do things I don't want to." Jo looked at her brother and shook her head sadly.

The quick bowler was too much for Tylan to handle. He missed two balls, nearly played on to a third and then he got a wicked bouncer and ducked straight into it. Tylan went down and Kiddo rushed on to the field immediately. But before Kiddo reached him

Ty was on his feet and rubbing the back of his head. He was swaying about a bit and you could tell he was still groggy. After a moment or two, he and Kiddo walked off together, Kiddo carrying his bat.

Marty faced one ball from the fast bowler which he didn't seem to pick up all and it whistled by his off-stump.

Now my thoughts were beginning to turn to Ohbert. Could we let him go out and face fast bowling of this quality? He'd be massacred. Perhaps we should call it off with the fall of the next wicket.

Matthew was now facing the spinner with just four overs to go. We still needed 56 runs – so there was no chance of a victory. Perhaps he could bat out the rest of the innings and save Ohbert from his fate. He came down the pitch to the ball and drove it past mid-on for two. But two balls later, he went back to one that shot out of the rough and he was bowled. Matthew had scored 26 and held the innings together almost to the end.

As he walked off he was met by Ohbert making his way to the wicket. Should I rush out and stop him? But then I saw Ohbert putting on Matthew's helmet and forearm protector.

"Ohbert's got his helmet on back to front," said Azzie.

"That's how he wears his baseball cap," said Frankie. "It won't make any difference to his batting anyhow."

Marty helped him to adjust the helmet and Ohbert squared up to the spinner. It was an unequal contest. The first ball missed his bat by an enormous distance; it spun across his wicket, just passing leg stump. The next ball was pitched in the rough again and Ohbert played a sort of scoop shot. The ball ran up his arms and bounced off the keeper and went for two runs. Then he went rushing down the pitch and kicked the next ball away for a leg-bye to bring up our hundred. It also gave Ohbert the strike against the pace bowler from the bottom end.

But now something very strange was happening. Great crowds of people were flowing into the ground. There were men dressed in flashy shirts and women in bright coloured dresses and great big summer hats. It was as if the whole island had got to hear of

Ohbert's innings and was flooding in to see him. They gathered around the boundary and watched as the fast bowler raced in and bowled. It was short and fast and going just over his head when suddenly Ohbert caught sight of it. Instead of ducking he aimed his head at the ball – a perfect header. Crack – it glanced off the front of his helmet and sliced through the slips for four leg-byes. Ohbert watched it go and then took off his helmet and rubbed his head. The crowd loved it; they laughed and cheered and applauded.

"My helmet!" moaned Matthew.

"What's his name?" asked a large woman in a pink dress.

"Ohbert," said Frankie. "He's a bit of a head case."

Again Ohbert faced the fast bowler. This time he got a yorker in the block hole. Ohbert tried to get out of the way but as he danced about the ball caught the toe of his bat and deflected just past the leg stump for four more. The crowd roared.

"Good shot, Ohbert," shouted the woman and a few more people caught up the name and started chanting, "Ohbert, Ohbert."

Now the bowler was getting angry. He was beginning to look foolish and he roared in with another furious bouncer. Ohbert rose like a swan and tried to head it again but this time it was too high for him; it ballooned over him and the keeper and it went for four byes.

"Ohbert, Ohbert," the cry went up. There were tears of laughter running down people's faces. Frankie was almost hoarse with shouting and cheering and even Clive was shouting Ohbert's name.

Fourth ball. Just short of a length and Ohbert played his immaculate forward defensive – one of the two great shots in the Ohbert repertoire. The crowd gasped at the strangeness of his shot selection. Ohbert had no idea where the ball was, of course, but it lobbed off the handle off his bat, looped over the desperately diving keeper and went for two more runs.

The next ball was a fast, full toss. Ohbert was perfectly in line, then he lifted his bat high and let the ball go through. The middle stump cartwheeled out of the ground. There was a low groan from the crowd but then they applauded and cheered. "Ohbert, Ohbert," sang the woman in pink, dancing on to the pitch and waving her hat over her head. Ohbert stood terrified as she advanced towards him.

Kiddo waved to Marty that the game was over. The doctor had had a look at Tylan and said he might be a little concussed. Everyone agreed that there was no point in him batting again. He looked okay but he had a bit of a headache.

So the game was lost and we clapped the Carlton players into the pavilion.

"What are all these people doing here?" asked Marty as he walked in with the hero of the hour.

The large woman smiled. "We've come for the open-air prayer meeting – but Ohbert was much more fun," she said.

Ohbert handed the helmet to Matthew who quietly examined the dent on the top of it.

BATSMAN	RUNS SCORED	HOW OUT	BOWLER	SCORE
1 M. ROSE	1.2.1.2.2.1.1.1.2.3.2.1.1.1.2 1.2	bowled	BABBS	26
2 C. SEBASTIEN	4	ct HILLABY	WILDEY	4
3 A. NAZAR	4.2.1.3	ct BENTHAM	WILLIAMS	10
4 C. DA COSTA	2.2.1.4.1.1.1.4.1.3.2.1.2.2.2 4	bowled	BABBS	33
5 E. DAVIES	1.1	ct BENTHAM	BABBS	2
6 H. KNIGHT		bowled	BABBS	0
7 T. McCURDY	2	ct ALLEYNE	MULLINS	2
8 F. ALLEN	2.4	ct CLARKE	BABBS	6
9 T. VELLACOTT	-	RETIRED	HURT	0
10 M. LEAR		NOT	OUT	0
11 P. BENNETT	2.4.2	bowled	CHANCE	8

FALL OF WICKETS

SCORE	4	21	72	74	74	80	92	97	114	
	1	2	3	4	5	6	7	8	9	10
BAT NO	2	3	4	5	6	7	8	1	11	

BYES	1.4		5
L BYES	2.2.1.1.1.4		11
WIDES	1.1.1.1.1		5
NO BALLS	1.1		2

TOTAL EXTRAS: 23
TOTAL: 114
FOR WKTS: 9

SCORE AT A GLANCE

BOWLING ANALYSIS · NO BALL · WIDE

BOWLER	1	2	3	4	5	6	7	8	9	10	11	12	13	OVS	MDS	RUNS	WKT
1 B. WILLIAMS	M	M	2:·	W·. .22	·.4. ...	·1· 1·								6	2	13	1
2 B. WILDEY	·.4· W4·	·2· 11	4+· 3·.	·.· 1·1	·1·. 2·.	·1· ·4·								6	0	28	1
3 O. CHANCE	·:1 ·.1	2·1 ·.1	·.1 ··2		·1· ...	·4· 2W								4.5	0	16	1
4 M. MULLINS	·.: .3.	·2· 2..	2.0.4 1·..	·.. 0.4	·1· 2·.									6	0	20	1
5 G. BABBS	4W. ·1.	WW. ·.2	··2 ·1·	14W ·.4	2·W 2·.									5	0	21	5
6																	
7																	
8																	
9																	

Chapter Four

GLORY GARDENS' TOUR OF BARBADOS

Tour Itinerary		Result
Sunday, February 13	Carlton School	lost by 36 runs
Tuesday, February 15	Wanderers Bay	
Thursday, February 17	Yorkshire	
Sunday, February 20	Drax Mill College	
Tuesday, February 22	Griffiths Hall School	

Our timetable didn't leave us much time for sitting around on the beach. After the first game, we already knew this wasn't going to be a holiday. And now we had a growing injury list. Maybe I was getting too anxious but the fact was that one more injury would leave us with only ten players.

Jacky was definitely out for at least a week even though the X-rays showed there was no break. That meant the rest of us including Ohbert would probably have to play every one of the next four games. Tylan still had a bit of a headache after his knock but otherwise he seemed okay. But Frankie was wilting in the heat. After his torrid experience behind the stumps in the first game he'd been unusually quiet. He sat around in the shade drinking litres of lime soda and every time he came out in the sun his skin went red and blotchy.

"So tell me what went wrong yesterday?" said Jo. She always insists on a post mortem on every game we play – especially if we lose.

"If anyone says the word 'byes' I'm leaving. Bye bye," said Frankie. He was already red and sweating even though it was only 10 o'clock in the morning and the sun was nowhere near its hottest yet.

"The byes weren't the only thing. We didn't bowl and field like we can," said Cal.

"Perhaps we're just short of match practice," suggested Matthew.

"Or jet lagged," said Tylan.

"Erica and Hooker bowled okay," said Mack.

"And Cal," said Jo looking at her score-book. The three of them bowled 18 overs for 54 runs. The other 12 overs cost us 71."

"So what are we going to do? We've got another game tomorrow," said Jo.

"Chill out by the pool," suggested Frankie. The swimming pool was just in front of our chalets. Ohbert had been the first to discover it on the evening we arrived. He walked straight in at the deep end with his suitcase. After the splash all that could be seen was Ohbert's baseball cap bobbing on the surface – then Ohbert emerged choking and spluttering. He can't swim so Kiddo had to jump in and pull him out. His suitcase burst open and we fished out Ohbert's clothes one by one. You wouldn't believe the things he'd brought with him. Apart from his full range of revolting coloured tee-shirts and shorts, there were scarves and gloves and even three thermal vests. Ohbert must think Barbados is in the Antarctic," said Tylan.

Ohbert is sharing a 'chalet' with Frankie. They're not really chalets, more like huts with verandahs; each one has a bedroom and a tiny kitchen. I'm sharing with Cal; Marty and Azzie are on one side of us and Jo and Erica on the other. Kiddo's got the biggest chalet to himself at one end of the pool and Clive's aunt is at the other end although we never see her except at matches because she's always visiting friends and relations all over the island.

We make our own breakfasts in our chalets. Cal and I have cereal and fruit. You don't want to eat much because it's so hot. The fruit's great though – there are mangos, paw-paw, pineapples and all sorts of different bananas but my favourite is ugli fruit which looks ugly but tastes nicer than oranges which used to be my favourite.

Jo wasn't going to be put off by her brother's idleness. "We need a coaching session," she said firmly.

"There's nowhere to practise near here," said Clive who was no keener on the idea than Frankie.

"What about the beach?" said Jo. "I'll ask Kiddo."

Everyone except Frankie, Clive and Ohbert, who hadn't been listening, was in favour of Jo's idea and half an hour later we were by the sea, setting up our stumps in the hard sand. We used a tennis ball and when it got wet the bounce was exactly like yesterday's wicket at Carlton.

Kiddo had plenty to tell us about playing on fast, bouncy pitches. He concentrated first on Marty's bowling. You're trying to bowl too fast, kiddo, and forgetting to bowl variety."

Frankie lay down on the sand in the shade of a palm tree and pretended to fall asleep, sensing another lecture from Kiddo. "You see," continued Kiddo, "Everyone here bowls fast – most of them faster than Marty – but the really good bowlers are the ones that use their heads."

"Sounds hairy to me," said Tylan. "Don't they leave teeth marks on the ball?" Frankie snorted with laughter.

Kiddo pretended not to hear. "The trouble with bowling out here is that there's no grass. Most of the time you'll get no movement off the seam and precious little swing – but plenty of bounce. So what do you do?"

"Vary the length," said Marty.

"That's right, kiddo. But remember to keep your bouncer and yorker as surprise weapons. And you can vary your pace too, and your direction by using the full width of the crease. And another little tip . . ."

Frankie yawned loudly and Jo gave him a sharp kick so he ended his yawn with a little yelp.

". . . you can also begin your run up a bit further back so you release the ball a bit sooner. Understand?"

Marty nodded.

37

Marty normally bowls with his front foot level with the batting crease. Here he's a good bit further back as he releases the ball. The idea, as always, is to surprise the batsman.

At last we started playing properly and Cal and Azzie padded up. Kiddo had us all bowling at them and he told us to try and work out the differences in their batting.

Cal's tall and plays on the front foot with a high back lift. Azzie's the smallest player in the team – he plays the ball late with lots of wrist and, given half the chance, he'll get underneath it and hook.

"If you pitch it up too much to Calvin, he'll drive you," said Kiddo. "With his long stride and reach, a good length to him is a couple of feet further back than for Asif."

Kiddo said the biggest mistake most teams make when they come to Barbados is to try and play like the local teams as soon as they arrive. "Remember, they're used to the conditions, you're not. So, when you're batting, don't try and knock the cover off the ball. Just place it in the gaps in the field and try to be nice and relaxed."

"That's not easy when someone's bowling at your head at 100 miles an hour," said Mack.

A good length ball to Cal will be short for Azzie and he'll hook or pull it out of the ground

"I didn't even see my first ball yesterday," moaned Marty.

"That's a bit of a problem," said Kiddo. But then no-one – not even the best batsman – likes really fast bowling. So you've got to get in the right frame of mind. As the bowler runs in you should be thinking, come on, then, I've got a whole range of scoring shots waiting for you. And if you're relaxed you'll pick the short ball, or the over pitched one quickly and pounce on it."

We'd been practising for about 40 minutes when we noticed two boys standing and watching us from a distance. The taller one shouted to Cal. "Mind if we join in?"

"Can't see why not," said Cal. "What do you do?"

"I'm a bowler and he's a wicket-keeper," said the tall boy pointing to his friend who was doing stretching exercises and grinning broadly as if his face had got stuck in that position.

"We need a proper keeper. Do you want a game tomorrow?" Cal smiled mischievously at Frankie.

The 'wicket-keeper' grinned and nodded.

"What's your name?" asked Frankie.

"He's Galahad and I'm Curley," said the tall one.

"Then let's see if you can bowl, Curley," said Frankie. "And I'll show Galahad how to keep wicket." Curley measured out a shortish run and Frankie squatted down behind the stumps. Curley's arm came over in a blur and I didn't see the ball again until it bounced off Frankie's nose.

"Sorry," said Curley. "It was a bit short."

"Good thing it was only a tennis ball," said Frankie rubbing his nose.

Galahad grinned and spoke for the first time. "What about the long run, Curley?"

"Okay," said Curley. And this time he came in off about twenty paces. Frankie had gone back at least ten yards but the ball whistled past the off-stump and he didn't get a glove on it.

"Four more byes to Frankie," said Mack.

"Couldn't you just hit the wicket for a change, Curley," grumbled Frankie.

Then Galahad took over behind the stumps while Frankie batted. He was a busy keeper rather than a tidy one but he was lightning quick on stumpings. Every time you played and missed you'd turn to find Galahad smiling from ear to ear, hand raised high and the bails flying through the air.

We practised for nearly two hours and then it was so hot we were all ready for a swim. Frankie was close to melt down and he seemed to sizzle like a plump sausage as he hit the water.

"I think I'll stay here for the rest of the week," he said wallowing happily on his back in the gentle waves. But he didn't need any encouragement to leave for lunch.

"Good keeper, that Galahad," said Mack as we walked up the beach waving goodbye to the two friends.

"Too flashy and unreliable," said Frankie and he looked surprised when we all laughed.

Chapter Five

In the evening light it looked at first just like a typical English scene. There was the red brick school and the playing field with its white sight-screens and pavilion. But as you got closer you soon noticed that it wasn't very English at all – the school stood amongst palm trees and bright green parrots were flying over a lawn in front of the school where a big fire was glowing.

We'd all been invited to the barbecue at Griffiths Hall School and it was our first chance to see Thompson Gale, Victor Eddy, Cardinal Williams and the other Griffiths Hall players since we'd played against them at the Priory.

"How'd you get on against Carlton?" asked Thompson as soon as he saw us. It was pretty obvious from his wicked grin that he already knew the result of yesterday's game.

"If you can't beat Carlton, I wouldn't even bother to turn up at Wanderers," said Henderson Springer, their wicket-keeper. Our next game was tomorrow afternoon against Wanderers Bay – we'd already heard they were good.

"Wait till Vincent Haynes gets you in his sights," said Thompson. "He's already taken 40 wickets for Wanderers this season . . . and put two batsmen in hospital."

"He can't be faster than Richard," said Matthew probably remembering the screaming bouncers which had flashed past his nose in the World Cup final.

"Just you wait," said Thompson with an evil smile. Thompson Gale and Richard Wallace are the Griffiths Hall pace attack and the fastest pair of bowlers I've ever faced. It was difficult to imagine anyone much faster.

Frankie looked unimpressed however. "I can't remember much about Richard's bowling in the World Cup," he said. "Except for when I creamed him for four."

"All I can remember is that you had a lucky win," countered Thompson.

"Lucky! Since then we've become champions of England," protested Tylan.

"Yes. We've read all about it," said Thompson.

"In the newspapers?" asked Mack.

"No, Frankie's letters," said Thompson. "There wasn't much else in them. He went on and on and on about it."

"It was even better than thrashing you lot in the World Cup," began Frankie. According to Mack, Frankie was showing all the signs of turning into a vampire – sleeping most of the day and then bursting into life as the sun went down. He was unstoppable this evening and he launched off on the story of the great Edgbaston victory all over again and hardly stopped talking till the barbecue was ready. Then he went strangely quiet and stared lovingly at the mountain of hot-dogs, hamburgers, fried chicken, spicy chops and spare ribs.

"Don't mind if I start, do you?" he said, grabbing a fistful of sausages.

"Try some of this," said Thompson.

"What is it?" mumbled Frankie as he drowned a sausage in a bowl of evil-looking red sauce offered by Thompson and took a huge bite.

"Spitfire sauce," said Thompson. "It'll warm you up."

Great beads of sweat broke out on Frankie's forehead and his face immediately returned to its daytime, bright red colour. His eyes opened wide and tears ran down his nose. "Wow! That's unbelievable."

"I've been keeping it specially for you," said Thompson. Thompson had been on the wrong end of one of Frankie's more unpleasant practical jokes during the World Cup and he was enjoying his revenge. But it took more than a bowl of spitfire sauce to keep Frankie from his food. Gasping for breath and with the tears still pouring down his face, he tore into the chops and spare ribs.

Meanwhile I was catching up on the news of the Griffiths Hall team. Victor Eddy told me they'd had a good season in Barbados and finished second in their league.

Wanderers' Bay, the only team to beat them, had won the title. Griffiths Hall had a new captain since last season too, with Henderson, their keeper, taking over from Victor.

"Wanderers Bay are the best side you'll play – apart from us," said Victor. "But Yorkshire won't be an easy game. They're a strong bowling side, too."

"So that only leaves Drax Mill College," I said gloomily.

"They've got two players in the island side," said Victor.

"It's looking more and more like a 5-0 whitewash," said Thompson. "Never mind. Forget about the cricket and just enjoy yourselves. Relax."

"Great idea," mumbled Frankie – his mouth and hands were still stuffed full of spare ribs and the sauce was running down his arms. The spare ribs had definitely got Frankie's vote as the best thing on the barbecue menu and he seemed to be growing quite fond of the spitfire sauce, too.

"You'll be ill, Francis," warned Jo.

Frankie mumbled something incomprehensible and attacked another rib. Even Thompson was impressed with his performance. "His appetite's even bigger than I remember," he said.

"But even Frankie can't eat non-stop for a week," said Cal. "What's there to do between meals?"

"Scuba diving, tennis . . ." began Victor.

"What about fishing," said Thompson. "We could go out on Victor's dad's fishing boat."

"Pity I didn't bring my rod," said Tylan.

"I don't think it's the same as fishing on the canal," said Erica.

"If you can fish you can fish," said Tylan mysteriously. "What do you catch?" he asked Thompson.

"King-fish, dolphin."

43

"Disgusting," said Jo.

"Not dolphin like Flipper," said Thompson. We call them dolphin but they're more like . . . well, fish. Then there's flying fish and marlin and shark." Tylan's eyes grew wider and wider.

"I said it wasn't like the canal," said Erica. "When did you last catch a shark on a maggot?"

"How do you catch flying fish? In a butterfly net?" asked Frankie.

"Sometimes they just leap on to the deck of the boat and we cook them straight away," said Victor.

Frankie patted his stomach. "Sounds like my sort of fishing."

"I hope the sharks don't fly as well," said Mack.

"We could have a fishing competition," suggested Victor.

"Yeah, Glory Gardens v. Griffiths Hall," said Tylan.

Victor said he would organise the trip with his dad. The boat could take only ten of us – so there'd be five from each team. Frankie volunteered to be our team captain.

"You'll sink the boat if you eat another spare rib," said Cal but Frankie wasn't listening. As long as there was food to eat Frankie was there eating it. His feasting came to an end only when Kiddo said we needed an early night before tomorrow's game. There were a few groans but Kiddo remained firm. He said it would be early nights until we won and we all packed into the coach and left.

"I say next time we don't bring our teacher with us on tour," said Frankie.

"I think Kiddo's pining for Gatting," said Tylan.

"I wonder what Gatting's doing now," said Erica.

"Eating or sleeping," said Frankie. "That's all he ever does."

"Funny, that reminds me of someone," muttered Cal.

"He'll be fast asleep in the kennels," said Jo. It's 2 a.m. in England."

"And cold and snowing," said Cal looking out of the window of the bus at the sugar cane fields and the palm trees. It was then that I remembered my promise to send Lizzie a postcard every day and that my first one was already three days late. So when we got back I borrowed a card from Kiddo.

Barbados is the best place in the world, especially for swimming and cricket. Ohlbert fell in the pool with his suitcase and most of his clothes have shrunk. We saw everyone from Griffiths Hall tonight at a barbecue but I forgot to give your photo to Victor. So far we've played one game of cricket and I took two for 16. I bet you are missing me. See you, but not soon!

Harry

P.S - We are going fishing for shark and dolphin.

I didn't see much point in telling her any of the bad news like getting a duck or losing our first game or about Jacky's finger. In fact, I put everything in I could to make her think she was missing out on the holiday of a lifetime. In the end I quite enjoyed writing it.

The card showed a scene of our beach looking like a tropical paradise. I put a cross on it to show her where we go swimming.

Chapter Six

Wanderers Bay was one of the best cricket grounds I'd ever seen. It was quite small with bananas and coconut palms growing at one end and beyond them you could hear the roar of the sea and the cackling of the big blackbirds you find all round the coast.

We were all pleased to get there because our mini bus driver was completely mad and he drove at what seemed like 90 m.p.h. down little, windy lanes between the tall sugar canes. Frankie nearly threw up and Matthew was as white as a ghost when we arrived.

The ground had a wooden pavilion with a rusty corrugated iron roof and it was full of pictures of old teams and famous West Indian players. We were playing against Wanderers Bay's junior side, a club team like us.

The Glory Gardens line-up for the game picked itself:

Matthew Rose
Cal Sebastien
Azzie Nazar
Clive da Costa
Erica Davies
Hooker Knight
Mack McCurdy
Frankie Allen
Tylan Vellacott
Marty Lear
Ohbert Bennett

Jacky came along to watch but he was very quiet and, I think, a bit depressed that his finger hadn't got any better.

"If you win the toss, we'll bat," Frankie said to me. "I don't feel much like fielding today." It wasn't just the heat that was bothering Frankie; he was also suffering from last night's binge and an overdose of spitfire sauce. He was in luck because I lost the toss and they put us in. Vincent Haynes, the fast bowler everyone was talking about, was Wanderer's captain. He told me we were playing a 35-overs game today – he couldn't explain why sometimes they played 30 overs and sometimes 35. It meant that each bowler had a maximum of seven overs. Vincent looked pleased to be bowling – it was as if he could hardly wait to get at us.

"You'd better get yourself padded and helmeted up," I told Matthew who was looking a little anxious at the prospect of meeting the fastest junior bowler in Barbados.

"Never mind, Matt," said Cal. "It'll all be over soon enough and it's not too far to the hospital." Matthew smiled feebly, tightened the chin strap on his helmet and grimly walked out to bat.

It's not often that Matthew gets off the mark with a four off his first ball. He can only have picked up the short-pitched delivery from Vincent at the last split second and, involuntarily, he drew the blade of his bat up to his chest to protect himself. The ball caught the shoulder and flew over the slips to the boundary. Matthew watched it go and then casually practised a cut shot as if to say, that's the one I should have played.

The rest of the over brought a series of oohs and aahs from the Glory Gardens' spectators. Vincent was not just fast; he was fast, aggressive, dangerous and he seemed to have pace to spare. And when he bowled a lightning, in-dipping yorker, none of us picked it up at all. Matthew coped pretty well, jamming down his bat and taking a single as the ball bounced out towards the covers.

The bowler from the other end was over six-foot tall – he even made Cal look small. He was nowhere near as quick as Vincent but his height made him awkward to play. He got a lot of bounce and Cal had a job to pick the length and play his normal front-foot game. Finally, out of frustration, he went for one outside the off-stump and got a thin edge to Vincent who was fielding at first slip.

Azzie came in with the score on 10 for one.

Az had been very disappointed with his innings at Carlton – he'd got in, then got out. He always seems to enjoy the challenge of a really quick bowler and so today there was a bit of extra edge about his batting from the very first ball which he glided down past square-leg for two.

But the real fun started when Vincent bowled at him from the other end. The Wanderers' quickie tried to greet Azzie with a very pacy yorker but he slightly overpitched and was astonished to see the ball coming back in the opposite direction travelling twice as fast. Before he could even get a foot to it the ball flashed past on its way to the boundary. Vincent turned and stared. Four runs to Azzie.

"What's the bet the next one's a bouncer?" said Frankie who was a little more cheerful although he was still bright red and his stomach was making loud gurgling noises.

"It won't be a leg break," said Tylan.

"More likely a break leg," said Frankie with a grin.

Azzie ducked as a short-pitched ball reared at him and it went harmlessly through to the keeper. The next delivery was also short and this time Azzie pulled. He didn't get it quite off the middle of the bat but it went well enough to give him two more runs. Another boundary off the last ball – a full-blooded cover drive – meant that Azzie had take 10 from Vincent's over. Vincent didn't look at all happy about it.

Matthew remained at the other end blocking and nudging and so, when Vincent returned to the attack, it was to continue his duel with Azzie. This time he went for eight runs, although he beat Azzie twice with two practically unplayable balls – one of them went straight over middle stump.

With eight overs bowled we had scored 37 and Vincent took himself off. "First round to Azzie," said Cal.

"I think he's waiting to bowl at Frankie," said Tylan.

"He'll have an easy target," said Cal gesturing at Frankie, who was eating again: this time he was wading through an enormous bunch of bananas.

"Want one?" asked Frankie, throwing the smallest of the bananas at Cal.

"But you've only just had lunch, Francis," sighed Jo.

Azzie continued to take the attack to Wanderers. The new bowler was another quickie and Azzie twice cut him to the cover-point boundary. The ball was coming on so well that anything short or overpitched had four written all over it. Azzie brought up our fifty with an enormous six hooked over the fielder at backward square-leg. A startled parrot flew up as the ball landed.

It began to look as if we were heading for a record-breaking score. Azzie was going like a train and Matthew was doing the job he likes best – holding up an end and letting the other batter score the runs.

"Azzie's on 49," announced Jo. It didn't seem possible – he'd only been at the crease for a matter of minutes. But now suddenly the runs dried up again – a couple of overs went by without Azzie seeing much of the strike. Still he needed one for his fifty.

There was another change of bowling and on came a left-arm spinner at the banana tree end. Azzie launched into his first ball and it went straight back over the bowler's head, one bounce, into the bananas. The whole Wanderers Bay team applauded the fifty. It had been one of Azzie's best and it made me feel really proud of Glory Gardens. After a quick wave in our direction Azzie settled down to face the next ball. Again it was pitched up and Az went for a repeat of the previous shot but this time he got it a bit too high on the bat and it flew in the air to extra-cover. The fielder took it well at head height. The applause had scarcely died down for his fifty and now Az was walking back to the pavilion.

Jo said Azzie's 53 had come off 46 balls – it had been a great knock and he raised his bat high in reply to the applause from both teams as he trotted up the pavilion steps.

"Beat that," said Cal to Clive.

"Leave it to me," said Clive strutting out to the wicket.

As if to prove it, he hit his second ball through the covers for four. But then disaster struck – off the last ball of the over, Clive was given out lbw as he went for a sweep shot. The ball may have

Catching a ball at head height can be difficult if you let your hands block your view. Move your head slightly to one side to keep your eyes on the ball and as you catch the ball let your fingers 'ride' with it taking the pace off it.

straightened on him, but to be honest it looked as if it was going down the leg side. Of course, like all great batsmen, Clive is never out. You could tell from his body language that he knew that the umpire had made a big mistake and we braced ourselves for the big moan when he got back to the pavilion.

I didn't have to listen for long because a dreadful misunderstanding between Matthew and Erica left Erica stranded in the middle of the pitch and I was in.

As I took my guard I tried to get my last disastrous innings out of my brain. One of the tricks I use to help my concentration is to focus on the score. We were 81 for four and there were nearly 20 overs remaining. I set out my stall for us to score at three or four an over to begin again.

I was soon off the mark with a couple of runs from a check drive on the off side. The ball went a lot further than I expected and if we'd run the first one hard there might have been three in it. The shouts from Cal and Frankie on the boundary showed that they thought so, too.

I felt pretty comfortable against the spinner and the first-change bowler at the other end wasn't really giving me any trouble either. The runs came steadily and, when the spinner dropped short, I pulled him for my first boundary in Barbados.

Then Vincent made another bowling change. He came back himself at the same end as before. I did a rapid calculation. He had three overs left. Should I block him out and pick off the spinner at the other end? Or give him the Azzie treatment?

The first ball had me sparring helplessly outside the off-stump; I'm not sure I even saw it before it was through me. The next thundered into my pads but fortunately it was going just down the leg side. Then, with my eyes adjusting to the pace of the ball, I got one in my half of the pitch and I drove on the up. The feeling as it connected with the meat of the bat and sped away on the off side was amazing. I didn't bother to move – nor did the fielders – it was four all the way to the extra-cover boundary.

"Now try one with your eyes open," said the keeper, bringing me back to earth with a bump.

The score-board stood at 99 for four. And I played out the rest of the over – not comfortably but at least I was now seeing the ball. There's something about playing a really fast bowler. I can't say it's fun but it gets your adrenalin flowing.

It was Matthew who brought up the 100 with a typical Matthew nudge. His total contribution so far was 18 – but that didn't matter at all. He'd hung in there against the fastest bowling he'd seen in his life and kept it out while the runs flowed from the other end. In his own way he'd made a great start to the series.

I faced up to Vincent again and leg-glanced him off my thigh for two. Next I ducked under a quick bouncer and then came the yorker. I thought I'd got my bat on it but it dipped into me in the last fraction of a second and Vincent was appealing almost before it rapped into my pads. No doubt in the umpire's mind either – his finger shot up. Mack met me as I was half way back to the pavilion.

"What shall I do?" he asked.

"Get your bat in the way," I said.

"By the way, Frankie's not feeling too good. A few too many bananas, I think," said Mack over his shoulder. He lasted just two balls against Vincent before his middle stump did a cartwheel and it was Frankie's turn to face the music. I hadn't a chance to ask him how he was feeling but as he got up to bat I noticed he was looking rather green through the blotchy red bits.

"I'm too young to die," he groaned.

"You're nearly 14," said Jo. "That's quite old."

"I wish we had two helmets," he muttered, his voice trailing off as he walked away from us.

Vincent greeted him with a bouncer. Frankie poked at it with his bat and the ball flew to the keeper's left for two fluky runs. Now Matthew played the next six balls from the spinner and, rather cruelly, I thought, refused a quick single off the last ball. So Frankie was again left with the strike against Vincent.

He started playing him by numbers. One step back and heave, then one step forward and swing. Three times he missed completely; one hit him high on the thigh and had him jumping about and then the keeper conceded a couple of byes. Finally Frankie got it right. He stepped back towards square-leg and swung wildly at a short, lifting and very fast deliver and it rocketed off the middle of the bat past cover point's despairing dive for four.

Two balls later Frankie played a similar shot to one pitched up on his middle stump and missed. The bails flew high in the air and Frankie's brief ordeal was over. And so, thankfully, were Vincent's seven overs.

With nine overs to bowl and seven wickets down, Matthew took charge, farming the bowling as much as he could and trying to make sure we batted out the full 35 overs. Since the first ball he received he hadn't hit another boundary which was quite an achievement on a small pitch with a lightning outfield. Still he progressed steadily with one and twos and the Wanderers players must have been beginning to get fed up of the sight of him.

Vincent continued to ring the bowling changes but nothing could faze Matthew; he clung on like a limpet. Normally Frankie and Clive would have given him plenty stick for slow scoring but Frankie wasn't in the peak of form and he was looking at the round, red bruise on his thigh and Clive was still complaining about his lbw decision. It would have been unfair to criticise Matt anyway – without him we would most likely have been all out by now.

With a few strokes of luck Tylan did what was needed and they were both still together when the final over began – the score stood at 140 for seven. Tylan was so confident now that he drove the first ball into the covers. And then Matthew struck out at the bowling for the first time. The luck stayed with him and he slammed the final ball of the innings over mid-wicket for four to end and begin his innings with a boundary.

He'd scored 47 not out. "What a shame," said Azzie as he clapped in the two unbeaten Glory Gardens' batsmen. "If only I could give him three of my runs."

We'd made 151 for seven.

INNINGS OF GLORY GARDENS   TOSS WON BY WAN.D. WEATHER SUNNY.

BATSMAN	RUNS SCORED	HOW OUT	BOWLER	SCORE
1 M. ROSE	4·1·1·2·1·1·3·1·1·1·1·1·1·2·2·1 2·1·2·1·2·2·1·2·1·(38)2·2·1·4	NOT	OUT	47
2 C. SEBASTIEN		ct HAYNES	LEONE	0
3 A. NAZAR	2·1·4·2·4·2·4·2·4·4·1·6·1·1·1 4·2·4·(49)·4	ct HASTINGS	GREENIDGE	53
4 C. DA COSTA	4	lbw	GREENIDGE	4
5 E. DAVIES		RUN	OUT	0
6 H. KNIGHT	2·1·2·1·4·4·1·1·2	lbw	HAYNES	18
7 T. McCURDY		bowled	HAYNES	0
8 F. ALLEN	2·4	bowled	HAYNES	6
9 T. VELLACOTT	1·1·2·1·1·1·1	NOT	OUT	8
10 M. LEAR				
11 P. BENNETT				

FALL OF WICKETS											BYES	2·2	4	TOTAL EXTRAS	15
SCORE	10	17	81	81	105	105	115				LBYES	2·2·1·1·1·1·1	9	TOTAL FOR	151
BAT NO	2	3	4	5	6	7	8				WIDES	1·1	2	WKTS	7
											NO BALLS				

SCORE AT A GLANCE

BOWLER	BOWLING ANALYSIS · NO BALL + WIDE														OVS	MDS	RUNS	WKT
	1	2	3	4	5	6	7	8	9	10	11	12	13					
1 V. HAYNES	4· ·1	M	4·2· ··42	2·	X	··4	2·w w2·4	··	X						7	1	35	3
2 D. LEONE	1·· 2·1	·w ···	·24 ···	·· ·1	··6 ·4·	3· 4··									7	0	26	1
3 J. CLIFF	4· ·41	1· 1··	·2	1· 2·1	·1 ·!		X	·1 ··1	X						7	0	24	0
4 R. GREENIDGE	4w· 4·w	··2 4··	·1 ·1·	1· 1·2	··2 ··1	M	X								7	1	24	2
5 T. MONCREIFFE	··2 ·1	·2· 1··	·· 2·1	1· 1·	122 114										5	0	23	0
6 C. HASTINGS	··2 ··1	2· 11													2	0	6	0
7																		
8																		
9																		

Chapter Seven

"It's a really short boundary on the leg-side. I can't see how we're going to defend 150," said Marty, always the optimist.

"Just bowl them out and I'll worry about the fielders," I said. I'd decided to stick to the same speed/spin combination of Marty and Cal to open our bowling. There wasn't much doubt that Wanderers would go on the attack and, if we got lucky with our catches, we might rock them back with a couple of early wickets.

The sight of Frankie behind the stumps didn't fill me with confidence. He wasn't looking at all well. He was sweating buckets and every now and again his face would twist and distort into the most horrible shapes as he creased up with sharp stomach pains. I was expecting him to rush off the field at any moment. I put Cal down at fine long-leg for Marty's bowling – more as a back-stop than to save runs off the bat.

Marty's first over went for eight runs thanks to two loose deliveries down the leg side but Cal dropped quickly into his line and length and, if an easy catch had gone to anyone else except Ohbert, we'd have been off to a flier. Ohbert ran in so fast when everyone shouted, "Catch!" that the ball went clean over his head. He tried to pirouette and catch it in mid-air but fell in a twisted, crumpled heap. The batsmen were so surprised by the performance that they forgot to run an easy single.

"Ohbert, you complete airhead," snarled Cal. "Why don't you look at the ball?"

"Oh but, my legs couldn't stop running," whimpered Ohbert.

"Next time tell them to stand still, Ohbert," I said.

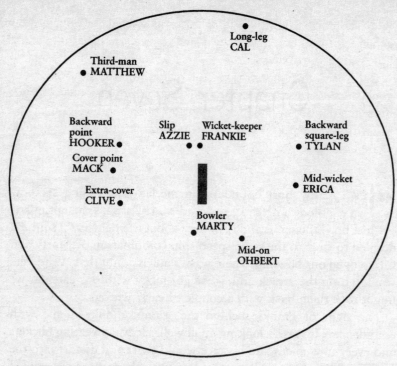

Marty bowls to a fairly defensive field

Marty bowled a better line with his next over and twice he found the edge. The first dropped just short of Azzie at slip; the second was a technical chance to Frankie but it flashed through high to his right and he didn't even get a glove on it.

Our luck got worse. Cal had a big shout for lbw turned down; it looked pretty adjacent to me even though I was fielding at mid-wicket. Then Matthew put down a spiralling catch deep on the long-on boundary. In the next over Marty himself missed a sharp caught and bowled – it was going like a rocket and he was completely off balance, but I've seen him take catches like that plenty of times.

Whenever a few chances go begging morale starts to flag and it's a big problem to pick everyone up again. I kept clapping my hands and shouting, "Come on Glory Gardens. Pull yourselves together."

But it did no good. Little fielding mistakes started creeping into our game; vital runs were given away and everyone was getting wound up – Cal, in particular.

Cal's been my closest friend for years. He's the best: generous, good fun and he knows loads about cricket. But his one problem is his temper. It doesn't happen very often, but now and again he goes off with a big bang. A few moments later everything will be okay again but it's best to be well out of range when you see the warning signs.

In Cal's fourth over nothing went right. He had another close lbw appeal turned down; then Frankie let a bye through his legs and Azzie misfielded at mid-wicket and gave away a couple more runs. There was another lbw appeal off the fifth ball – though this time Frankie didn't join in the shout – and the umpire turned it down again. And then he called Cal for a no ball for over-stepping.

Steam was almost coming out of Cal's ears as he ran in to bowl the final delivery of the over. It was driven straight back at him and Cal picked up, turned and threw at the stumps at the bowler's end. The ball flew at head height straight at the umpire who just managed to get his hand up in time to stop it hitting him smack in the face. The ball had been thrown so hard it bounced out to me at mid-wicket. It was an accident but Cal didn't apologise to the umpire; it was the end of the over and he stalked off to his fielding position at long-leg.

Hands on hips the umpire watched Cal making his way to the boundary. You could see he wasn't happy and he went over and had a word with his opposite number at square-leg who wrote something in a notebook.

Eventually the game continued with the score on 40 for no wicket. I didn't know what to do about the Cal incident . . . so I did nothing. Instead I tried hard to concentrate on the game. I decided it was time to rest Marty – he had been quite expensive – and I took over from him myself. My first ball was glanced down to Cal who came in off the boundary, picked up and threw wildly – the ball must have gone ten feet over Frankie's head and if it hadn't been for a brilliant tumbling dive by Clive, running round and backing up, it would have gone for four overthrows. This time it was my turn to stare at Cal.

"Relax, Cal," shouted Frankie. He'd have probably said a lot more if he'd been feeling better.

"You couldn't catch it if I threw it straight at you," snapped Cal.

I was about to go over and have a word with him when I noticed Kiddo walking round the boundary. I guessed he was going to speak to Cal – Kiddo hates it when anyone loses their cool in a game.

With relief I got on with the bowling and I soon forgot all about Cal because my second ball moved away off the seam, took an outside edge and Azzie completed the catch at first slip. At last we'd got a wicket.

At the end of the over Cal and Kiddo were deep in conversation on the boundary. Kiddo seemed to be doing most of the talking and Cal was nodding and looking serious. The game stopped for a few minutes as we watched and waited for Cal to continue the bowling. Eventually he walked in from the rope, went straight up the umpire and said something. The umpire smiled and took the cap that Cal handed to him, then they shook hands.

"Okay?" I asked Cal as I walked back with him to his mark.

"Yeah. I had a bit of a brainstorm, but it's okay now."

"What did you say to the umpire?"

"Just 'sorry'. I was surprised he took it so well. I was a bit out of order." I smiled to myself – it was typical of Cal. "Can I have square-leg out?" he asked, as if to say end of subject let's get on with the game. The last ball of his over brought the biggest appeal yet for lbw. Everyone went up for it except Cal who was down on his knees, begging for the verdict. The umpire looked at him, smiled and raised his finger.

"Yeah!" bellowed Cal raising both arms in a victory salute.

We'd got ourselves back in the game at 46 for two but Wanderers' opening bat, Dilip Rajah, was scoring quickly and looking ominously in control, especially against me. After bowling three of my overs without feeling I was going to get another wicket, I went for a double bowling change – Cal had just finished his seven

58

over spell. Erica replaced me and Tylan continued the spin attack.

Tylan didn't start too well – a wide first ball and a full toss which was cracked for four. It was probably overconfidence which brought the batsman's downfall: he played an awful head-in-the-air shot and gave Tylan an easy caught and bowled. 75 for three – after 16 overs.

As usual Erica put a break on the run scoring, while Tylan was fairly expensive – so it sort of balanced out. But our performance in the field was still letting us down badly. Perhaps it was the strange sight of a subdued Frankie or maybe we still hadn't got used to the fast outfield. But that didn't account for the dropped catches. A couple more went down: Mack of all people just failed to hold on to a low, diving chance in the covers. Nine times out of ten you'd expect him to take a difficult catch like that. Then Ohbert dropped another sitter off Tylan. This time he just had to step forward a pace to catch it but he stood stock still and the ball bounced up and hit him on the knee.

"Ouch," said Ohbert.

"Why didn't you move, you oaf?" said Tylan.

"Oh but, Hooker told me to stand still," Ohbert grinned at me.

I didn't bother to say a word. It was a lost cause.

Steadily the game was running away from us. Dilip Rajah brought up his fifty and the Wanderers' hundred with a lovely four driven through the covers. The runs were coming too fast and I decided that Tylan had taken enough stick and I played my last card – I brought back Marty.

I had no choice but to go on the defensive with the fielding positions. Wanderers needed only 39 from 11 overs and with seven wickets left they were odds-on favourites. That, of course, meant no slips and the risk of denying the bowlers that extra chance of taking the wickets we needed so badly. Bowling now from the banana tree end, Marty seemed to get a touch more help from the pitch. He bowled the number five batsman with a no ball and had a couple of edges through the vacant slip area.

I forced myself to think positively. A big over from Marty could still change everything. Erica bowled a maiden and Marty came back. He was putting every ounce into it and working up a lot of pace. A fast yorker just got a faint inside edge – otherwise it would have been leg before middle stump. A chinese cut went for two and then, at last, he produced the knockout blow. Dilip Rajah went back to cut a ball just outside the off-stump and he got a thin bottom edge on to his wicket. Although I joined in the applause I was delighted to see the back of him. Every one of his 56 runs had felt like a nail in our coffin.

Erica grabbed a deserved wicket in her last over – trapping the new batsman lbw for a duck.

Her seven overs had cost us only 15 runs for one wicket and, with Marty, she'd pulled us back into the game. Now there were eight overs to go and Wanderers still needed 31. But my big headache was, who was going to bowl them? Marty had one left; I had four. I didn't

Erica bowls a surprise in-cutter which traps the batsman on the back foot. The in-cutter (or off-cutter) is delivered with an arm action similar to the out-swinger – that's why it's such a good surprise ball. Erica bowls it sideways on and then pulls her fingers across the seam at the moment of delivery like a fast off-break.

want to risk Tylan with so few runs to play with – so it would have to be Mack or Clive. I decided to go for Mack – he'd bowled atrociously in the Carlton game but then he'd only had one over.

Marty fired out another of the Wanderers' batsmen with a lovely in-swinger and suddenly we were amongst the tail-enders and they weren't looking quite so confident. The new batsman was their captain Vincent Haynes.

I bowled to five fielders on the off side, aiming to pitch on or outside off-stump and stop them going for the short, leg-side boundary. By keeping the ball pitched up I got driven hard into the covers a couple of times but there were only four runs off the over.

Mack was hammered for four over mid-off, second ball, but he settled down after that and at the end of the thirtieth over they were 134 for six. It was going to be a tight finish.

Vincent drove the second ball of my next over into the covers and ran. He might have been a fraction slow off the mark but Mack certainly wasn't. He picked up left-handed and with a flick of the wrist his skidding throw to the bowler's end easily beat Vincent's spectacular but hopeless dive. He was run out for two.

Now it all depended on which team could keep its nerve. The coolest player on the field seemed to be their number five batsman, Jeffrye Cliff. He kept the runs flowing with ones and twos, calling sharply and precisely. In between overs, he walked down for a long chat with the batsman at the other end – pointing out the gaps in the field and talking him through his nerves. I couldn't help thinking back to the easy catch that Ohbert had put down off him.

With three overs left they needed just 10 to win and Ohbert dropped his third catch, this time off my bowling. It was hit straight at him and fairly hard. For a moment it looked as if he'd done the impossible and caught it, but the ball spun out of his hands and he juggled with it for ages before it finally fell to the ground.

"Good try, Ohbert," said Azzie.

I didn't feel like saying anything especially when Ohbert said, "Sorry, Hooker, I'll get it next time."

Frankie gave away two more byes off a tidy last over from Mack.

He wasn't looking well and he let out a low groan as the second one went through him. I couldn't help feeling sorry for him, even though it was all his own fault he was sick.

And so I began the last over. They needed just three runs. There was a single off my first ball and then at last Frankie took a catch behind the wicket. He nearly threw up when Cal slapped him on the back to congratulate him. I brought all the fielders in for the new batsman who pushed the next two balls straight to them. Jeffrye Cliff came down the wicket for another conference. They needed two off two.

I bowled on off-stump and the batsman managed to push it to Ohbert. Jeffrye was through for the run as Ohbert picked it up at the third attempt. They could probably have run two to him as we shouted and screamed at Ohbert to get it in.

With the scores level I had two choices: bowl a perfect yorker or try and beat the bat outside the off-stump with an away-swinger. I went for the second choice. It was a bit wide and Jeffrye cut in the air. Mack dived at cover point but it was just out of his reach. Four runs. We'd lost – on the last ball of the match.

I was the first to congratulate Jeffrye and Cal shook hands with the umpire who told him he had a good throwing arm and laughed loudly.

The Wanderers hospitality after the game partly made up for our disappointment – the food was even more brilliant than at the Griffiths Hall barbecue except for the fried yams which I didn't like very much.

"It's the best grub we've had since we arrived," said Cal pushing a chicken leg under Frankie's nose. "Try it, fatman." Frankie groaned and turned his head.

Soon we'd almost forgotten how we'd thrown the game away with our terrible fielding and Ohbert's three missed catches and everyone except Frankie was talking happily to the Wanderers' players.

"You're not related to Wyckham Wanderers, are you?" Tylan asked Vincent.

"Who are they?" said Vincent shaking his head.

"Our biggest enemy in England," said Tylan. "If you ever meet someone called Liam Katz, please don't tell him we were beaten by a team called Wanderers. We always beat them, don't we Frankie?" Tylan looked round for Frankie. He was sitting on his own on the verandah of the pavilion with his head in his hands looking very sorry for himself indeed.

BATSMAN	RUNS SCORED	HOW OUT	BOWLER	SCORE
1 W. LAMMING	4·4·2·1·1·2·2	ct NAZAR	KNIGHT	16
2 D. RAJAH	1·3·2·1·4·1·1·2·2·1·1·1·2·1·2·1·2·4 1·2·1·4·(40)1·2·1·4·4·1·1·2	bowled	LEAR	56
3 E. CONSTANT	2·2	lbw	SEBASTIEN	4
4 R. GREENIDGE	1·1·1·4·2	c & b	VELLACOTT	9
5 J. CLIFF	1·1·2·1·2·2·1·2·2·1·2·3·2·1·4·1·1 2·1·2·(34)1·2·1·4	NOT	OUT	42
6 T. MONCREIFFE		lbw	DAVIES	0
7 E. HASTINGS		bowled	LEAR	0
8 V. HAYNES	1·1·	Run	OUT	2
9 S. PHILLIPS	1·1·2	ct ALLEN	KNIGHT	4
10 C. HASTINGS	1·	NOT	OUT	1
11 D. LEONE				

FALL OF WICKETS											BYES	1·2·1·1·2·1·1·1·2·1·	14	TOTAL EXTRAS	21
	1	2	3	4	5	6	7	8	9	10					
SCORE	4+	46	75	118	121	124	135	150			L BYES	1·1·1·1	5	TOTAL	155
BAT NO	1	3	4	2	6	7	8	9			WIDES	1	1	FOR	8
											NO BALLS	1	1	WKTS	

SCORE AT A GLANCE

BOWLER	BOWLING ANALYSIS · NO BALL · WIDE													OVS	MDS	RUNS	WKT
	1	2	3	4	5	6	7	8	9	10	11	12	13				
1 M. LEAR	·4· ·43·	··· 3··	··4 1·2	·22		··2 ·12	·1· 2W·	·3· W·1						7	0	34	2
2 C. SEBASTIEN	·1· ··1	··2 1·2	·11 11·	··· 2·0·	·1· 2·W	··2 ··11	·1· 11·							7	0	22	1
3 H. KNIGHT	1W· 12··	··2 1··	·12 4··		·12 ·1·	1·· 2·1	··1 ·2·	1W· ·14						7	0	30	2
4 E. DAVIES	··2 ···	1·· 1··	·1·2 1·2	4··	··1 2·1	M	·2· W··							7	1	15	1
5 T. VELLACOTT	·4· 2W·	··4 ·11	·1·2· ·21	·2· ·41										4	0	24	1
6 T. McCURDY	·4· ··1	··2 1·1	·2· ·2·											3	0	11	0
7																	
8																	
9																	

Chapter Eight

"Where's Dracula this morning?" asked Mack. It was long after breakfast and there was no sign of Frankie at all.

"I think he sucked something last night that didn't agree with him," said Cal. We all filed into Frankie's bedroom to take a look at him. It wasn't a pretty sight.

"I think I died in the night," Frankie moaned. His face had changed colour again – now it was yellowy green.

"He's turning in to a banana," said Tylan examining Frankie closely.

"A banana would be more useful," said Cal. "Did you know you've let through 30 byes in two games on this tour, fatman?"

"And how many runs have you scored, Mr Opening Bat?" Frankie asked Cal in a croaky voice. "Four, isn't it?" There was still a little bit of fight left in him after all.

"I think he should go into quarantine," said Azzie.

"It's okay, he's only sharing with Ohbert. Ohbert can't catch anything – he's not human," said Tylan. Ohbert was sitting on his bed listening to his Walkman. He didn't seem to have noticed that we had all invaded his bedroom.

"Ohbert, we're going to lock you away with Frankie," shouted Tylan. Ohbert looked up and grinned.

"I . . . I think I'm going to be sick," moaned Frankie. And we all rushed out of the chalet.

"If he's not better tomorrow we'll be down to ten players," said Marty.

"Well I know where we can find a wicket-keeper," said Clive. We all looked at him. "Galahad," he said.

"Galahad who?" said Marty.

"You know, Galahad and Curley – the two we met on the beach."

"And how do you imagine you're going to find him again?" asked Cal. "You can't go around asking everyone in Barbados if they've seen Galahad."

"I bet I can find him," said Clive.

"He won't want to play for us," said Marty. "He's probably got his own team."

"Just leave it to me," said Clive. And perhaps Curley will play, too – instead of Ohbert."

Jo immediately leapt to Ohbert's defence as usual: "Ohbert wasn't the only one to drop a catch. I counted seven of them."

"Three by Ohbert," murmured Clive.

"And what about his batting in the first game," said Mack.

"He makes us look like the biggest joke side in Barbados," said Clive dismissively. "If that's what you want, it's okay with me. But I'm going to find Galahad."

Frankie didn't emerge from his chalet for the rest of the day. Occasionally Ohbert would appear with an order for another bottle of water. "Are you sure he wouldn't like some bananas or a spicy spare rib, Ohbert?" asked Cal.

"Oh but, I'll ask him," said Ohbert.

"I should stand well back and wear your raincoat, Ohbert," said Cal.

After lunch Kiddo sent for a doctor who said that Frankie was suffering from acute food poisoning but he'd be fine in a day or two. It was looking more and more likely that he'd miss the next match.

That afternoon Erica, Tylan, Mack and Azzie played tennis, Clive went off with his aunt to visit some of their relations and Ohbert stayed behind to look after Frankie. The rest of us went to the beach. Kiddo got hold of some masks and snorkels and we saw some amazing fish swimming about really close up. It was strange to think that they were there all the time when you were swimming only you couldn't normally see them. The coral was fantastic too –

wonderful shapes and colours which sparkled in the sunlight – and there were black sea eggs which Kiddo said were deadly if you trod on them.

It was time to write another postcard to Lizzie.

POST CARD

I'm sitting under a palm tree drinking a coconut. You drink them first and then they split them in half with a machete and you scoop out the white stuff which is still soft – not like the ones you get at home. Delicious! I've just been snorkelling and seen loads of amazing fish, miles better than the ones in your fish tank. You can swim right up to them before they get frightened. Frankie's got food poisoning from eating to many spare ribs and bananas. I got 18 in the last match and took two wickets. It's getting better and better

Harry

PS - You can borrow my long scarf if it's really cold.

I had to write extremely small to get it all on the card but I was quite pleased with it when I'd finished, especially the bit about the fish tank – Lizzie's calls it her aquarium but it's only little, with three weird-looking fish and a snail. As I thought of her reading the card I smiled to myself.

There was more bad injury news when we got back to the chalets.

Tylan was lying by the pool with his ankle bandaged, sipping a large Coke through a straw.

"He tried to get my baseline lob back and he made a big mess of it," said Azzie.

"I think it's just a sprain," said Erica, "but it's definitely swollen."

"We'd only played one set. And we were winning, too," complained Mack.

"I bet he won't be able to play tomorrow," said Marty going straight for the bad news like a terrier. A closer inspection of Tylan's ankle by Kiddo suggested that Marty might be right. It was red and very swollen.

"We'll have to wait and see what it's like in the morning, kiddoes," said Kiddo.

The bulletin on Frankie hadn't improved either. Ohbert emerged in his raincoat to fetch another bottle of water and told us he'd been sick again.

"I hope Clive finds Galahad," said Cal. Because it looks as if we're going to need Curley as well against Yorkshire."

"I wonder if they'll all have names like Geoffrey Boycott and Darren Gough," said Tylan.

"Who?"

"The Yorkshire players."

"Don't be silly," said Cal.

"Then why are they called Yorkshire?"

"I don't know. Ask them tomorrow."

We didn't hear any more from Clive that evening. There was a message later from his aunt that they were staying overnight with some cousins and they'd meet us at the Yorkshire game.

———————— • ————————

Yorkshire turned out to be a village in the middle of the island. It took an hour to get there, driving flat out along the bumpy, little lanes. We flashed past signposts to places with names like Newmarket, Brighton and Windsor.

We still hadn't heard from Clive about Galahad. Tylan said that he would play if we were desperate but he was still hobbling about and it was obvious that he wouldn't be able to bowl properly and he'd be practically useless in the field.

Frankie was still in bed – he looked a bit better today but he still wasn't eating anything – and Jacky's finger was still too painful even to hold a cricket ball. He came along to support us but he was still very quiet.

"What will we do if Clive doesn't find us a keeper?" I asked Kiddo.

"Perhaps Yorkshire will lend us one of their players, kiddo, and we can play ten a side," he said. I wasn't very impressed with that idea – but I couldn't think of a better one.

There was no sign of Clive when we arrived at the ground. Nothing unusual about that as Clive is always late – but it didn't make things any easier. The pitch looked a bit rough, especially the outfield. There was a cow tethered in one corner outside the boundary. "That must be the lawn mower," said Tylan.

I changed very slowly. I was in no hurry to tell the Yorkshire captain that we had only eight fit players on the ground . . . and one of them was Ohbert. Partly to slow things down I put a new grip on my bat handle.

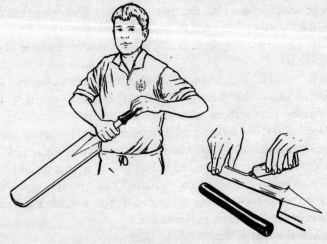

Keeping your bat in good condition is really important. A worn or split grip can be a distraction – enough to cost you your wicket. Replace the grip regularly.

Then one of the umpires put his head round the changing room door and told us to get a move on.

I was out in the middle tossing up when I saw Clive and his aunt arrive in a taxi. Galahad got out of the back of it, followed by Curley; they were both carrying their kit.

"Forget everything, we're back to full strength," I said to Walter Heddings, the Yorkshire captain. I'd only just finished telling him about our injury list.

"That's a quick recovery," he said, baffled by our sudden change of fortune.

Clive came rushing out to speak to me with a broad smile on his face. I hadn't seen him look so pleased with himself since he scored fifty for the Colts. "I found him, Hooker," he said. "And guess what? Curley's here, too. Isn't that lucky – because Cal says Tylan's out. I asked him to come in case Ohbert fancied a rest."

"Not Curley Johnson," said Walter spotting our latest recruit on the boundary.

"Do you know him?"

"Yes, he's a good cricketer. If you can get him to play, that is."

Clive watched me lose the toss and, after Walter elected to bat, he said suddenly, "Why are you called 'Yorkshire'?"

Walter grinned. "By 'eck, lad. 'Cause Yorkshire's where us comes from, int'it?"

"Is it?" said Clive, completely fooled by Walter's amazing accent. Walter shook his head. "No. It's the name of the village. I suppose the first settlers came from Yorkshire."

"Oh," said Clive looking a bit embarrassed. He turned away and shouted to Galahad. "Get your keeper's pads on. We're fielding."

"So what kept you?" I asked Clive. "We'd almost given you up."

"We only found Curley and Galahad half an hour ago. You can thank my aunt for tracking them down. You wouldn't believe how many people she knows in Barbados."

At last the match was about to begin.

Chapter Nine

I suppose I should have let Curley open the bowling with Marty. I knew he was quick and an early wicket would have fired him up. The pitch was hard and bumpy, too – ideal for fast bowling. But I decided to stick to the speed/spin formula of Marty and Cal which had worked fairly well for us so far. Also, I wanted Yorkshire to get a taste of the real Glory Gardens players before we brought on our 'guest' bowler.

In his first over Marty got one to fly off a length; the ball just brushed the opener's gloves and Galahad took it cleanly behind the stumps. He did a little jig, threw the ball in the air and then roared out a deafening appeal. When he got the decision he jumped over the stumps, loped down the pitch and bounced on top of a terrified Marty, throwing his arms around him. Galahad then did a lap of honour round the infielders handing out 'high fives' before returning to his place behind the stumps to resume his grinning.

Next ball Marty's in-dipping yorker had the new batter groping in front of his stumps and the umpire didn't take a moment to give him out lbw.

Galahad was off again on his 'high five' circuit, an even bigger smile lighting up his face. With the arrival of the number four batsman he set about geeing everyone up for Marty's hat-trick. "Keep it bubbling," he chirped. "Pressurise him." The new batter tapped the hat-trick ball calmly back down the pitch and this time there was a big groan from behind the stumps. "Unlucky, Marty, unlucky, man," cried Galahad.

But if Galahad was like a rubber ball full of pent-up energy,

Marty bowls the perfect yorker. Before the new batsman has got his eye in and his feet moving, he bowls an extra quick delivery swinging into his legs and pitching on the crease.

Curley was just the opposite. He was so laid back that I felt I was waking him up each time I told him where to field. He even made Ohbert look alert. A force on the leg side went straight through him for four and then he didn't bother backing up Mack's shy at the stumps and it cost us four more. Cal was the bowler to suffer on both occasions; the first time he just glared at Curley but after the overthrows he couldn't keep his thoughts to himself any longer. "Why don't you get your towel and do a spot of sunbathing?" he said to Curley.

Curley shrugged. "You bowl rubbish, you get hit for four," he murmured turning his back on Cal.

"What did you say?" demanded Cal. He was on the verge of going ballistic again. This time Azzie intervened. He walked all the way back to his bowling mark with Cal, talking all the time and looking up at Cal who is twice his height. Cal seemed to calm down a little.

I remembered what the Yorkshire skipper had said about

motivating Curley. How was *I* going to do it? Should I say, "Hey, Curley why don't you wake up and try a bit harder" or "Sorry, I've made a big mistake; you should have opened the bowling."? One thing was certain, though, I couldn't ignore it. There was going to be a big row if I did.

Kiddo's always saying that the best captains get the best out of their players. The trouble is that all players are different. When Marty's not bowling well you have to coax him along and tease a performance out of him. With Cal you can say, "You're bowling more rubbish than our dustman," and he'll immediately try to show you you're wrong. But that approach doesn't work with Marty . . . or Tylan for that matter. If you're too critical of Marty's bowling it knocks his confidence. Tylan likes to have a bit of advice about what he's doing wrong but, more often than not, you have to calm him down because he can easily get over-excited when he's bowling.

Once you get to know players you begin to understand what makes them tick. But I didn't know a thing about Curley, so I decided the best thing was just to keep him in the picture. I told him he'd be bowling after Marty's spell at the top end. I made up the excuse that I thought there'd be more in the pitch for the quicks that end.

"I'm ready when you're ready," he said casually.

Marty was bowling too well for me to take him off. After beating the bat more times than I can remember he finally got one to find an edge and Azzie took a good catch at first slip. The next over he took his fourth wicket. This time the batsman swung across the line and a high catch went straight to Clive at mid-wicket.

Then Cal chipped in with a smart caught and bowled and we had Yorkshire looking down the barrel on only 30 with their top five batsmen back in the pavilion.

It was then that I decided to introduce Curley into the attack.

Curley grabbed the ball and his first delivery was dug in half way down the pitch and soared over the batter's head. Galahad had to leap out of his skin to stop it going for four byes. "Whoa, Curley," he shouted. "Get it in this half."

"Pitch them up," I said to Curley. The uneven bounce is on a length. There's no point in bowling short on this track."

Curley's next one was even faster and shorter and the batsman hooked it in the air – although he got a top edge it still went for six. Cal looked at me. "If you bowl rubbish you get hooked for six," he said. I began to wish I hadn't taken Marty off.

After another short delivery which was prodded away for a single, Galahad strolled towards me in the gully. "If you don't want him to bowl like this all day, tell him you'll take him off if he pitches another one short," he said.

"Will he take any notice of me?" I asked.

"You'll see."

I was too late to stop Curley's fourth delivery flying past the batsman's nose but I immediately strode up to him and said, "One more short one and you're off."

Curley stared at me for what seemed like a lifetime. I stared back without blinking. Then he turned and walked back to his mark. The next ball was a toe-crunching yorker which missed the leg stump by a fraction of a millimetre. Galahad took the ball and winked at me. From then on Curley bowled like a dream; in his second over he had both batsmen jumping around and at last he got his reward when one of them played on.

"What have you done to Curley?" asked Cal at the beginning of the next over.

"Nothing."

"Then why did he start bowling like a headless chicken and suddenly he's almost unplayable?"

"It's a funny old game," I said with a shrug and Cal turned to begin a new over. He tossed up a tempting off-break outside the off-stump and the batsman went for it. The inside edge flew in the air high and hard to Curley's right at mid-wicket. He took off like a greyhound and snatched the ball out of the air.

"Brilliant catch," shouted Cal and he rushed over and hauled Curley to his feet.

Cal finished his six-over spell with a third wicket – this time Galahad was the hero with a fine bit of stumping. The batsman just lifted his back foot and the bails were off before you could blink. Galahad went whirling round the pitch again like an electric hare. This time he got Ohbert in his sights and headed for him with hands raised high. A look of terror came across Ohbert's face and he ran off in the opposite direction. Galahad chased him all round the ground with Ohbert squawking in alarm.

At 47 for eight it looked as if we'd got Yorkshire exactly where we wanted them and I decided to bring Marty back at Cal's end to finish the job. But instead, with a few powerful blows from their number seven, Sealy, and one or two lucky edges, we suddenly found the score had rocketed up to 70 without another wicket falling.

Both Mart and Curley were bowling fast and on the target but the batsmen rode their luck and the runs flowed.

"What shall I do?" asked Cal.

"Pack the leg-side field and pray," he suggested unhelpfully.

"Or maybe bring on Erica?" I said.

"Maybe," said Cal thoughtfully. "It's a pity we haven't got another spinner in the side to give us a bit of variation."

Marty bowled his sixth and final over; it cost us only three runs and Galahad spilled a hard catch driving away to his left. Mart finished with four for 23. Curley kept up the pressure with an equally tight over and then Erica came on and bowled an immaculate maiden – trust Erica to respond with exactly what we needed.

Curley, at last, got the breakthrough but he needed a big helping hand. Ohbert was fielding a bit closer in than he should have been at mid-off – you can't keep an eye on Ohbert's position all the time and he wanders about like goldfish in a bowl. Curley's delivery was slightly overpitched on off-stump and the batsman drove low and hard and straight at Ohbert.

"Catch!" yelled Curley. The ball homed in on Ohbert like a scud missile and I saw his eyes open wide with horror. At the last moment he turned his back on it and tried to duck. It hit him square on the rump and rebounded. Ohbert yelped. Curley turned and dived. And the ball dropped into his outstretched right hand.

All of us, the batsman included, stood mesmerised.

"What a back pass," shouted someone from the boundary.

"I bet you've never been caught out and bowled like that before," said Mack to the batsman, who wasn't very amused. Galahad was out of his blocks and raced over to congratulate Ohbert who was rubbing his bruise. This time Ohbert stood his ground. "Oh but, go away, Galahad," he said irritably. "I don't want to be bounced. I've got a sore bum."

Erica took one more ball to finish the innings. It brushed between pad and bat and knocked over the off-stump. Galahad grinned as he caught the bail and threw it in the air. We'd finally dismissed them in the twentieth over for just 77 runs. But, as Cal said, "That was 20 runs more than we should have let them get."

Jo agreed. "Well bowled," she said. "Shame you let them off the hook at the end."

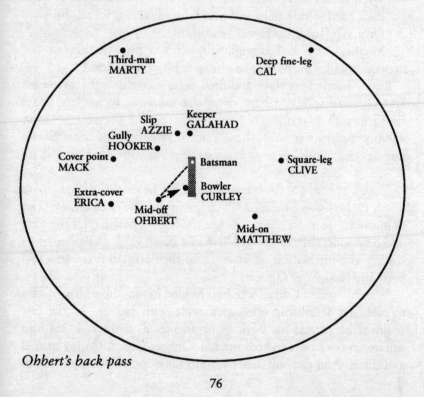

Ohbert's back pass

HOME TEAM	YORKSHIRE	V GLORY GARDENS	AWAY TEAM	AT YORKSHIRE	DATE FEB.17.TH

INNINGS OF YORKSHIRE   **TOSS WON BY** YORKS. **WEATHER** SUNNY

BATSMAN	RUNS SCORED	HOW OUT	BOWLER	SCORE
1 B. JOSEPH	1·	ct JONES	LEAR	1
2 S. LORD	1·4·4·1·2·2·1·1·1·1·2	c & b	SEBASTIEN	20
3 E. CHEFFETTE		lbw	LEAR	0
4 T. BAXTER	1·1	ct NAZAR	LEAR	2
5 A. COLE	4	ct DACOSTA	LEAR	4
6 R. MERRICK	1·	bowled	JOHNSON	1
7 N. SEALY	6·1·1·1·4·4·4·2·2·2	c & b	JOHNSON	24
8 W. HEDDINGS	1·	ct JOHNSON	SEBASTIEN	1
9 F. HOLDER	4	st JONES	SEBASTIEN	4
10 B. LASCELLES	2·1·2·3·1·2·1·1	NOT	OUT	13
11 A. HENRY	1·	bowled	DAVIES	1

FALL OF WICKETS												BYES	—	0	TOTAL EXTRAS	6
	1	2	3	4	5	6	7	8	9	10		L.BYES	1·1·1·1·	5	TOTAL FOR	77
SCORE	2	2	20	28	30	41	43	47	76	77		WIDES				
BAT NO	1	3	4	5	2	6	8	9	7	11		NO BALLS	1	1	WKTS	10

SCORE AT A GLANCE

BOWLING ANALYSIS · NO BALL + WIDE														OVS	MDS	RUNS	WKT
	1	2	3	4	5	6	7	8	9	10	11	12	13				
1 M. LEAR	·11 W·	·2 1W·	·· W·	1·4	X	·2· 3·4	·· 21·	X						6	0	23	4
2 C. SEBASTIEN	·4· 4·1	·2· 1·1	··· ··	W· 111	X	W· 4·W								6	0	23	3
3 C. JOHNSON	·61 ···	W· W·1	··· 2·1	·12 4·2	X	··· ·2	·12 W·1							6	0	26	2
4 E. DAVIES	M W													1·1	1	0	1
5																	
6																	
7																	
8																	
9																	

Chapter Ten

"Where have Jacky and Tylan gone?" Cal asked Jo.

"Fishing," she said. "They went off with Thompson and Victor."

"In Victor's boat?"

"I don't know," said Jo. "I just saw them arrive and then Ty and Jacky rushed off. They didn't invite me."

"Typical. Just when we need some support," said Marty gloomily.

Jo wrote down the batting line-up in the order I gave it to her. I'd decided to bat Galahad and Curley at six and eight and I dropped myself to seven:

Matthew Rose
Cal Sebastien
Azzie Nazar
Clive da Costa
Erica Davies
Galahad Jones
Hooker Knight
Curley Johnson
Mack McCurdy
Marty Lear
Ohbert Bennett

Kiddo's verdict on the pitch was, "A bit dodgy." He wasn't impressed with the uneven bounce. "If you get a couple of steeplers off a length you might find 77 is quite a big hill to climb, kiddo. So don't burst a boiler and think you can rattle them off in six overs." I got most of the message and I told Cal and Matt to take it steady – not that Matthew's ever likely to do anything else.

To make things worse the wind was getting up and the ball started swinging about alarmingly. Matthew plays the swinging ball well. He doesn't have much of a back lift and he lets the ball come on to him and plays it late.

Matthew watches the ball all the way. By playing it late he has time to see that it is swinging away and leave it outside the off-stump. If he had been drawn into a shot he would have probably given a catch to the keeper or slips.

At the other end Cal was less certain; he played and missed quite a lot and a couple of edges went through the slips.

"I wish Cal would stop fishing outside the off-stump," said Azzie as the ball again squeezed off an edge between first slip and the keeper.

"Was that the 'dab' or the 'plaice'?" said Mack.

"More like the 'flounder'," said Marty.

The fish jokes got worse and worse: "time we got our skates on"

. . . "Cal seems a bit out of tuna" . . . "the umpire needs a herring aid" . . . Fortunately I can't remember most of them. But there was a lot of laughing and groaning and no-one was paying much attention to the cricket.

Matthew and Cal were going along steadily when, in the fifth over, Matthew got a horrible delivery from the Yorkshire captain, Walter Heddings. It pitched on a length, spat off the pitch and cut into him sharply. Matthew went up on his toes and tried to fend it away but the ball lobbed off the handle of his bat to first slip who only had to stand and wait for it to fall into his hands.

Azzie then played a loose drive at his first ball and got an inside edge on to the stumps. "Bowled hook, line and sinker," said Mack.

Clive only just managed to dig out the yorker which would have given Walter his hat-trick. But two balls later he ran Cal out. He called him for a single and then, realising he wasn't going to make it, stopped and sent him back. Even if he hadn't slipped Cal would have had no chance of making his ground.

Then Clive was given out lbw to a ball which we all thought was going over the stumps. Of course, Clive thought so, too. He was glowing white-hot with anger when he came back. "I'm giving up this stupid, waste-of-time game. You can't play with rubbish umpires," he said and went off to sulk in the changing room.

"And he didn't even say sorry for running me out," said Cal with a wry smile.

I looked at the score-board and then at Jo's book just to convince myself it had really happened – we'd slumped from 14 for none to 15 for four. All of a sudden we were in a big hole.

Erica and Galahad tried to dig us out but the conditions weren't getting any easier. They both faced a succession of tricky deliveries; Erica calmly as usual, Galahad playing and missing a lot but looking quite unbothered about it. He'd picked up six streaky runs when he played and missed once too often and over went his leg peg. He strolled off smiling at everyone as if the best thing in his life had just happened.

"Make them suffer, Hooker," he said to me with a broad grin as I made my way to the wicket. I had four balls of Walter Heddings' last over to face and I set my mind of seeing him off. A lucky edge off the third ball went through the slips for four – the first boundary of the innings.

30 for five – I saw the figures go up on the score-board. I remembered that Yorkshire had been on exactly the same score. That means we can still get 77, I told myself.

"Plenty of time," I said to Erica, at the end of the over.

"But not much batting left," she said. "Unless one of us makes a score, we're going to lose again."

"No we're not," I said. "If Frankie were here I'd have a bet on it."

"At least we haven't got to watch him swinging at everything with his head in the air," said Erica. She got her head down and played out a maiden and Walter then brought on a spinner at one end. He was a tall, gangling bowler called Barry Lascelles and he could certainly turn it. I'm sure I heard his first ball buzzing through the air – fortunately it pitched wide of off-stump and I got my front leg across alongside my bat. The ball leapt off the pitch and spun into my pad. The bowler appealed – but I was well outside the line of the off-stump. If he turns it that far I'd better get right to the pitch, I thought. The next ball was a half-volley and I drove it for four.

Somehow Erica and I survived the next three overs, but it was still a pitch which you could never really trust and, just as things were looking up, Erica got a brute of a ball which shot along the ground and she was adjudged lbw. Curley came in and tried to hit Barry Lascelles into the sea, which was at least ten miles away, but instead he managed to spoon a catch to mid-on.

Mack didn't look very confident against the spinner but he played the quickie at the other end well and brought the fifty up with a lovely straight drive.

Another drive, this time into the covers, was hit hard to the fielder and he fumbled it. Mack called for a single. I was on the back foot and I got a slow start. Never run for a misfield – those were the words that flashed through my mind as the fielder recovered, picked up and hurled the ball at the stumps. It hit the base of the off-stump and I was still a yard short of the crease.

That left Marty and then Ohbert to bat – and we were 54 for eight. I just couldn't see them rustling up 24 more runs against high quality bowling on this pitch.

Tylan and Jacky had returned from their fishing trip while I was batting. Victor and Thompson were with them. Tylan had caught a huge fish and he dangled it in front of me as I walked in. "We caught it off the harbour wall," he said. "It's a king-fish. I'm taking it back for Frankie's supper."

"It's only a small one," said Victor. "The big ones are further out to sea."

It looked big enough to me. "I bet it put up more of a fight than Glory Gardens," I said, looking glumly at the fish's sad face.

"It's not looking too good, is it?" said Victor.

"Looks like 3-0 with two to play," said Thompson. I ignored him and watched the spinner run in and bowl to Marty who played a complete air shot off his first ball. He swung the next high on the leg side and it fell safely between two fielders. I could see Marty had decided he wasn't going to survive long so he might as well get some runs on board as fast as he could.

A confident shout for lbw against Mack had us all holding our breath – but he was given the benefit of the doubt by the umpire. The score crept into the sixties. Marty's swings kept just eluding the fielders – two runs came from a prod over mid-on; two more from a top-edge that fell just short of deep square-leg. But no-one was surprised when his luck ran out and he skied yet another on the leg side and was pouched easily by mid-wicket. The ninth wicket had fallen on 66 – and only Ohbert stood between us and our third West Indian defeat.

In Matthew's helmet Ohbert looked even more like a creature from Mars than usual. "Oh but, I'm in, am I?" he said as he at last realised why everyone was staring at him.

"It's your moment of truth, Ohbert," said Cal. "Death or glory."

"Give 'em the long handle, Ohbert," said Galahad.

"Oh but, all right, Galahad," said Ohbert walking backwards towards the wicket looking at his bat handle and finally tripping over his bat. Then he waved at us and turned to face the Yorkshire bowlers. The spinner had two balls of his spell left. The first turned and passed inches over Ohbert's middle stump. The second turned even further and Ohbert aimed a bat and a foot at it. The foot connected and they ran a leg-bye.

Unfortunately that meant Ohbert kept the strike. Mack had a futile talk about tactics with him which only resulted in Ohbert charging down the wicket at the quick bowler. He missed the ball completely and kept running. Mack sensibly didn't try to send him back but went for the run. All the keeper had to do was to catch it and bowl down the stumps. His underarm throw missed by a kitten's whisker and Mack was safely home.

A fine, leg glance from Mack brought us two more but he couldn't rotate the strike at the end of the over and Ohbert faced up to the bowling again. The new bowler who replaced the spinner was a medium-pace seamer, although I don't suppose that made any difference to Ohbert's stroke selection. He wound himself up for a big swing at the first ball and got an inside edge past the stumps and the keeper; they ran two. Mack tried to keep it to a single but Ohbert wasn't to be denied his second run.

"Six to win, Ohbert. Can you do it in one?" shouted Galahad.

"Please get down the other end, Ohbert," muttered Marty. "I can't bear watching you bat." But we had to watch and Ohbert showed no sign of wanting to lose the strike. He played his immaculate forward defensive to a ball which flew just past his nose. The next was a no ball and it had his off-stump cartwheeling out of the ground. Ohbert started to walk off but Mack screamed at him to get back in his crease and he casually stepped back just in time to avoid being run out.

Two more misses were perfectly judged – one went over middle stump, the other must have grazed the off bail. Ohbert was not troubled but the Yorkshire players were tearing their hair out in frustration. Suddenly from the depths of his puzzling mind Ohbert remembered the reverse sweep. I'd seen him play it once before; it looks as if he's trying to turn himself inside out. This time he played it against the medium pacer to a ball going down the leg side. It was an impossible shot but somehow he got a top edge and the ball flew to the keeper's right, completely wrong-footing him, and although three fielders raced after it, the ball just trickled over the boundary for four.

The scores were level and the Glory Gardens players were dancing round the boundary – most of them doubled up with laughter. Victor and Thompson couldn't believe their eyes and Galahad nearly went into orbit he was so excited.

There was one ball left in the over and again Ohbert played the forward defensive. This time by sheer luck he picked the right length delivery and met it squarely in the middle of the bat. We clapped and clapped – Ohbert had survived the over and now Mack had a chance to score the winning run.

Mack played three cautious defensive shots. Each time Ohbert came charging down the wicket and Mack had to scream at him to get back. He needed all his concentration to play the bowler and keep an eye on Ohbert at all times. The fourth ball was driven hard straight to extra-cover. Ohbert was off like a rabbit and Mack saw that this time there was no chance of stopping him and he ran, too. The throw was hard and low at the bowler's end. It just missed the stumps and the bowler caught it and tried to flick it on to the stumps. For an agonising second it looked as if Ohbert wasn't going to make it but the ball slid by the stumps and our hero puffed home. We'd won – thanks to an amazing tail-end wag. Mack was not out on 10 and Ohbert had added six priceless runs.

Galahad raced out on to the pitch and hoisted Ohbert off the ground and on to his shoulders. Ohbert grinned through the grill of his helmet as we all clapped him in.

"Oh but, I had a bit of luck," said Ohbert.

"Only a bit," said Thompson, still shocked by the amazing victory.

The Yorkshire team soon got over their disappointment and joined in the stories of Ohbert's greatest moments on the cricket field.

"I've never played against anyone like him," said Walter Heddings.

"That's what everyone says," said Tylan.

"He was even worse last year," said Cal. "I'm worried that he's over-training and losing some of his natural skills."

As for the hero himself, he was plugged into his Walkman again and didn't hear a word that was being said about him.

INNINGS OF ..GLORY GARDENS......   **TOSS WON BY** YORKS. **WEATHER** WINDY.

BATSMAN	RUNS SCORED	HOW OUT	BOWLER	SCORE
1 M. ROSE	2·1·1·2	ct LORD	HEDDINGS	6
2 C. SEBASTIEN	1·2·2·1·1	RUN	OUT	7
3 A. NAZAR		bowled	HEDDINGS	O
4 C. DA COSTA		lbw	HOLDER	O
5 E. DAVIES	1·2·1·2·1·2	lbw	HENRY	9
6 G. JONES	3·2·1	bowled	HEDDINGS	6
7 H. KNIGHT	4·4·1·1·1·1·2·1	RUN	OUT	15
8 C. JOHNSON	1·	ct COLE	LASCELLES	1
9 T. McCURDY	1·2·2·2·2·1	NOT	OUT	10
10 M. LEAR	3·1·2·2	ct JOSEPH	LASCELLES	8
11 P. BENNETT	2·4·	NOT	OUT	6

FALL OF WICKETS

	1	2	3	4	5	6	7	8	9	10
SCORE	14	14	14	15	26	42	43	54	66	
BAT NO	1	3	2	4	6	5	8	7	10	

BYES	2·1·1	4
L BYES	1·1·2·1	5
WIDES		
NO BALLS	1	1

TOTAL EXTRAS	10
TOTAL FOR WKTS	78 / 9

SCORE AT A GLANCE

BOWLING ANALYSIS · NO BALL + WIDE ○

BOWLER	1	2	3	4	5	6	7	8	9	'0	'1	12	13	OVS	MDS	RUNS	WKT
1 W. HEDDINGS	··2 ··	2· ·1 ··	·1· WW·	·· ·2·	·· ·11	·2·W ·4·								6	0	17	3
2 F. HOLDER	1·· 1·2	··· 1·W	1·W ··	·3· ··	·· ·2·	M								6	1	12	1
3 B. LASCELLES	·4· ·1·	··· 1·1	W· ·2	·· ·2·	·3· ·W·	·22								6	0	18	2
4 A. HENRY	·1· W·1	·2 ··	1·2 ·2	1·· ··	·1· ·1·	··2								6	0	14	1
5 S. LORD	2○· ·4·													1	0	7	0
6 T. BAXTER	··· 1·													0·4	0	1	0
7																	
8																	
9																	

Chapter Eleven

"Where's the fish you caught yesterday, Tylan?" Frankie asked. "Jacky said it was a whopper."

"It was massive," said Tylan. "But I must have left it at Yorkshire. I put it under the steps of the pavilion to keep cool and . . ."

"And then you forgot all about it," said Jo. "Typical."

"Yeah. It's a shame. It was at least a ten pounder. I was going to cook it for your breakfast," said Tylan to Frankie.

"Shame," said Frankie unable to hide the look of relief on his face. He was better but not that much better.

"Is it still there – under the Yorkshire pavilion?" asked Erica.

"I suppose so," said Tylan.

Frankie chuckled. "Just think of the pong. They'll have something to remind them of Glory Gardens for months to come," he said. "It could have been worse, though – you might have left them a pair of your socks instead, Ty." Tylan has what he calls 'problem feet' and anyone who shares a changing room with him knows all about them.

Frankie had made a remarkable recovery. He was back to his old bouncy self, looking forward to the fishing party. "Forget that old fish, Ty," he said. "We'll catch loads today and they'll be twice as big."

Frankie's 'team' to represent Glory Gardens against Griffiths Hall in the big contest consisted of Tylan and Jacky, who were the only real anglers, and then me, Ohbert and Frankie himself. Tylan was still limping from his injury but he wasn't going to miss a day's fishing. I think Frankie chose Ohbert because he'd looked after him when he was ill. It was hard to imagine Ohbert fishing . . . although he couldn't be worse at fishing than he was at cricket.

But as a cricketer Ohbert was fast becoming the hero of the tour. His innings at Yorkshire was already a legend, and not only with the Glory Gardens players. News travels quickly in Barbados, particularly when it's about cricket. I've never been to a place where everyone's so completely mad about the game. For the Bajans cricket is a way of life.

"How's the great Ohbert today?" asked our cleaner when she came round to tidy up our rooms and she chuckled loudly when Ohbert blushed and patted him on the cheek.

It was the same with the man on the gate as we drove off to the harbour. "Well batted, Ohbert," he shouted. "I wish I'd been there to see it."

Of course Victor and Thompson had told everyone at Griffiths Hall School about our victory, too. "Here comes Ohbert's team," cried Henderson when we arrived at the harbour where Victor's dad's boat was moored.

"I suppose you'll be opening the batting now, Ohbert?" said Victor. Ohbert nodded his head violently to the sounds echoing around inside it. He didn't appear to have noticed Victor, the boat or anything that was going on.

"He's available on a free transfer – any time you like," said Frankie.

Richard Wallace and Gary Lomas made up the rest of the Griffiths Hall fishing party with Victor, Thompson and Henderson. Victor's dad welcomed us on board and he and Victor quickly had the boat's engine started and we made our way out along the mouth of the harbour, called the Careenage, to the sea. The boat was quite big and painted brightly in red, gold and green. It's name *Sir Garfield III*, shone out in gold letters on its side.

"What's that up the front?" asked Jacky, pointing to a pole with a sort of net hanging from it.

"You mean the 'bow'," said Victor . "Boats don't have fronts."

"It's a net for flying fish," said Henderson.

"Frying fish?" Frankie looked puzzled.

"Flying fish," shouted Victor over the roar of the engine.

"I suppose they just fly into it," said Tylan with a wink at Frankie.

"Sometimes," shouted Victor. "And with a bit of luck you'll see them."

"We've got six rods and plenty of bait," said Thompson; the engine was getting louder as we hit the sea. Each team will have three rods and will take turns to fish because there's not room for all ten of us fishing at once. The team that catches the most fish in three hours will be the winner."

"Does it matter how big they are?" asked Tylan.

"No, but they're usually quite large," said Thompson.

"They'd have to be to swallow this in one go," said Frankie, pulling a small fish out of the bait bucket. These are as big as Ohbert's pet rat."

"The best bait is live flying fish," said Victor."But we'll have to make do with these."

I nodded. Victor could have said anything he liked and I would have believed him. "What's the biggest fish you've caught on a line?" I asked.

"A 300lb blue marlin," he said casually "But, I did have some help from my father to pull it in."

Tylan's eyes opened wide. "We won't catch any of those today, will we?"

"No," said Victor. "It's not really the season for them and we'd have to go out a lot deeper to find marlin. I think the record for the biggest one's about 1,000 lbs."

"Is that heavier than Frankie?" asked Jacky.

"Heavier than five Frankie's," said Victor smiling.

We travelled out of the harbour and turned right down the coast and then out to sea. After a while Victor's father cut the engine and let the boat drift. "We'll try here first," he said handing out the rods and showing Ohbert and me how to fix the bait to the hook and the best way to fish. Tylan and all three of the Griffiths Hall team had already got their lines over the side.

It didn't take long to get the hang of it and soon I too was staring out at my line waiting for the slightest movement to show there was a fish nibbling at the bait. Ohbert took a bit longer to get underway. First he hooked his shirt and dropped the bait down his neck and then, once he'd discovered how to get the hook out, he stuck it straight back in his shorts. Soon his line was in such a tangle that Jacky had to help him unravel it.

For nearly an hour we all took turns but there was no sign of any fish at all. "I've seen more action in the canal at home," moaned Frankie looking out to sea and yawning. Even Victor and Thompson were growing impatient and Victor had just asked his dad to take the boat further out when Jacky let out a cry.

"I think I've got one," he shouted. "And it's enormous."

His rod was bending alarmingly and Jacky pulled at it with all his strength. Under instructions from Tylan he slowly reeled in the line. In his excitement he caught his bad finger against the reel and nearly let go of the rod. But he hung on and bit by bit he hauled it in. I could see the fish struggling and flapping its fins just under the surface. It was about the same size as the one Tylan had caught yesterday, only much prettier – blue and green with long silver fins.

"It's a dolphin," said Victor. "But only a small one." It looked big enough to me and it didn't look like any dolphin I'd ever seen. It was more like the shape of a huge goldfish. Victor's dad leaned over the side with his gaff and speared the fish under the gills.

"Oh but, doesn't that hurt?" said Ohbert suddenly. His eyes were popping out of his head almost as much as the fish's and he nearly jumped over the side when the dolphin landed on the deck next to him and started flapping and lashing about.

"I think we've hit a shoal," said Victor. He and Richard were both pulling at their lines as their rods bowed under the weight.

"Oh but I hope I don't get one," muttered Ohbert looking with horror at the gasping fish which was now lying in a large basket on the deck of the boat.

"Ohbert, I don't suppose it ever occurred to you that if you came fishing you might catch a *fish*," said Jacky.

"He won't if he doesn't put his hook in the water – unless he's trying to catch a flying fish," said Tylan. Ohbert had been 'fishing' for twenty minutes with his bait dangling over the side of the boat well above the water line.

"Give it to me," said Tylan snatching the rod. As he spoke I felt a pull on my own line. I leaned back and held the jolt of the fish as it turned and swam away. It nearly snatched the rod out of my hands. I took the strain and slowly, turn by turn, inch by inch, I pulled my first dolphin to the surface. It was a big one, too. The biggest so far.

Soon the shoal passed and, after all the excitement, it went quiet again apart from the noise of the fish flapping about on the deck and the waves slapping against the side of the boat. Griffiths Hall were winning the competition 6 – 4. We'd all caught at least one fish except Frankie and Ohbert. Victor's dad started up the engine again and we went a bit further out to sea where he said he thought we'd find some king-fish.

Ohbert plugged in his Walkman, turned up the volume and fell asleep. Frankie decided it was time to sing us a song he'd just made up – he called it a sea shanty:

We set out in *Sir Garfield III*
In the blue Caribbean Sea
Hunting the dolphin for tea.

Ty caught two and Victor three
Big ones, too as you can see
But there were none for me.
Victor's dad looked out to sea
"Fishing's mostly luck," said he
And I had to agree.

And it went on . . . and on.

As the boat chugged along Ohbert's line dangled in the water behind it. Everyone else had reeled theirs in. Ohbert slept with his rod held across his chest and his arms folded over it.

All was quiet and calm apart from Frankie's endless sea shanty and the waves lapping gently against the boat. Suddenly, Ohbert jerked upright, his eyes open wide in amazement. His rod seemed to have come to life in his arms and Ohbert took a firm and determined grip on it. The line reeled out at an alarming speed and then it stopped with a twang. The rod jerked again and Ohbert was pulled to his feet and with a little cry he disappeared in a somersault over the handrail. We rushed to the side of the boat in time to see the splash but no Ohbert. He had vanished under the waves.

We stared at the surface of the sea helplessly. Victor's father immediately throttled back, put the boat into reverse and we came to a stop. "Take the wheel," he said to Victor as he looked for a sign of Ohbert. There was nothing.

"What was that?" asked Tylan.

"Could have been a big bonito or a tuna or even a shark," said Thompson.

"A shark!" screamed Tylan and Jacky.

"Don't worry, it won't be a dangerous one," said Victor's dad calmly. He stood on the side of the boat, his eyes scouring the surface of the sea behind us. Suddenly he dived off and a split second later I saw Ohbert's head pop up about 20 metres beyond him. "There he is," shouted Frankie. "Ohbert, stay there. Don't go away."

Ohbert gurgled and waved his arms in the air. He was still holding on to the fishing rod. Victor's father grabbed him, turned him on his back and propelled him powerfully back to the boat as Victor reversed the boat slowly towards them.

As they reached us Victor thrust out the gaff for his father to grab. We all took hold of bits of Ohbert and pulled him aboard and soon he was splashing about on the deck next to the dolphin.

"Next time you go for a swim, Ohbert, wait for the boat to stop," shouted Frankie.

"What was it?" spluttered Ohbert. "It was ever so strong and fast."

"Only a shark," said Frankie. "If you'd hung on to it we might have won the fishing competition."

"Oh but . . . sorry Frankie. I tried but I think something broke." Victor inspected the rod. The line had snapped and there was no sign of bait or hook.

"If it was a shark it probably died of fright seeing Ohbert coming after it," said Tylan.

"I wonder if his Walkman's still going," said Frankie snatching the headset from the dripping Ohbert and putting it to his ear. It doesn't sound any stranger than usual," he said.

Victor's dad decided we'd had enough fishing for one day and he turned the boat back towards the Careenage. We were about half way back when Ohbert let out a little cry as a small silver fish flew past his nose. Suddenly the water seemed to be boiling with them. There were more than we could count, some of them leaping four or five feet in the air. One landed on the deck at Tylan's feet and then a couple more. Victor even managed to catch a few in the fishing net. "Good, flying fish for tea," he said.

When we arrived back we weighed all the dolphin. Mine was the biggest and Jacky took a photo of me holding it up by the tail. Victor and his dad cleaned all the fish and then they grilled the flying fish in the ship's galley and we all sat on the deck eating delicious fresh flying fish sandwiches and talking about our adventure.

"The whole school's coming to watch the game on Tuesday," Victor told me.

"And we've got a surprise for you, too," said Henderson.

"Loads of food, I hope," said Frankie.

"Yes . . . and Carnival."

"What's Carnival?" asked Frankie through a mouthful of flying fish.

"Carnival's a big festival in Trinidad. We don't celebrate it in Barbados like they do there. But, since you can't go to Trinidad, we're going to give you a taste of genuine West Indian Carnival at Griffiths Hall."

"We're having a fancy-dress procession and a fair," said Richard.

"It'll make up for your disappointment when you lose the match," said Victor.

"I'm sorry to tell you that we've hit a winning streak," said Tylan.

"Winning streak!" scoffed Thompson. It was the luckiest win I've ever seen. And you needed two West Indians in your team to get a result."

"Can you imagine losing to an English team in front of the whole school?" said Victor. "It's too embarrassing to think about."

"We won't mind if you beat Drax Mill, though," said Henderson. "We've never liked them much."

Drax Mill college were our next opponents. Victor said we should watch out for a batsman called Wayne Carew who held the under-13s record for the most sixes in a season and Andy Laycock, a spin bowler and batsman; they both played in the Barbados team.

"But you've nothing to worry about as long as Ohbert's playing," said Richard.

"I know. And to think we nearly lost him to a killer shark," said Frankie.

Later that evening I wrote another card to Lizzie:

```
┌─────────────────────────────────────────────┐
│                          POST CARD          │
│                                              │
│   I caught a dolphin today all on      ·     │
│  my own and it weighed 21 lb. Ohbert   ·     │
│  was pulled off the boat by a          ·     │
│  shark but it got away after           ·     │
│  dragging him out to sea. I bet        ·     │
│  you've never eaten flying             ·     │
│  fish - you don't know what you        ·     │
│  are missing. Tylan's twisted his ankle ·    │
│  but Marty took four wickets           ·     │
│  at Yorkshire and we won by            ·     │
│  one wicket.                           ·     │
│          Harry                         ·     │
│  PS. Dont worry, dolphins aren't real  ·     │
│  dolphins they're just like ordinary   ·     │
│  fish only bigger. I'll show you the   ·     │
│  photo of mine when I get home.        ·     │
└─────────────────────────────────────────────┘
```

I don't know why I wrote the P.S. – I must be getting soft.

Chapter Twelve

What a difference a win made. I was really looking forward to Sunday's game against Drax Mill School. Things looked better on the injury front too. Jacky was still out but he could move his finger more easily and he said it was a lot less painful, in spite of the rainbow colours. Frankie was back with a vengeance; noisier than ever. Tylan's ankle seemed to have improved too but he was still limping. Curley Johnson kept coming round to see how he was and telling him he shouldn't risk playing until he was properly fit. Curley seemed to have taken a real liking to Glory Gardens; he'd even learned a couple of Frankie's songs and he was dead keen to play for us again.

In the end it wasn't so much Curley's persuasion as the promise of another fishing trip with Victor and his dad which helped Tylan to make up his mind.

"I'll be okay for the Griffiths Hall game, though," he said.

"Just make sure you catch Ohbert's shark," said Frankie.

———————— • ————————

Sunday afternoon was hot and sultry. After a quick inspection of the Drax Hall pitch, which looked a beauty, I won the toss for the first time on tour and had no hesitation in batting. I made a couple of changes to the batting order. Mack had looked in good form in the last game with his match-winning knock, so I decided to give him a chance to open; Cal didn't mind batting at seven, so I pushed Curley up the order too. That left me at eight, the lowest I'd ever batted for Glory Gardens, but I wanted to be there at the end of the innings in case we needed some quick runs.

Matthew Rose
Mack McCurdy
Azzie Nazar
Clive da Costa
Curley Johnson
Erica Davies

Cal Sebastien
Hooker Knight
Frankie Allen
Marty Lear
Ohbert Bennett

"Is it always this hot here?" sighed Frankie, slumping down next to Curley to watch the opening over.

"There'll be a storm later," said Curley. "We'll be lucky to get the game finished."

The new opening combination of Matthew and Mack started well and Matthew again showed how to deal with some lively bowling on a fast track. He even cut one for four in the third over.

"Steady on, Matthew," said Frankie. "What do you think this is? A 30-over slog? Get your head down and imagine it's a five-day test match."

"I think you all criticise Matthew too much," said Jo, rising to the defence of our white-helmeted opening bat. "Look at his scores on this tour. Do you know he's averaging 26?"

"Is that 26 hours?" asked Marty. A nicely timed on drive from Matthew brought two more runs.

"He likes playing on these pitches where the ball's coming on to the bat," said Erica.

"Perhaps we should leave him here then," said Frankie.

"That's 30," said Jo. We had reached the end of the seventh over and now Wayne Carew, their skipper, introduced a spinner into the attack.

"I bet this is Andy Laycock," I said. Victor says he plays for Barbados."

The spinner's first ball pitched outside Mack's off-stump – Mack bats left-handed like Clive – and it turned square across him. Mack's lunge forward missed the ball by a long way and it glanced off his front pad. There was a big appeal and fortunately, in the end, the umpire agreed with us – that Mack was well forward and probably outside off-stump.

"He's a leggie," said Cal. "I wish Tylan were here to watch him. He might learn how to bowl leg spin properly."

"Three guesses what Mack's going to do," I said. Mack belongs to the if-you-don't-understand-it-hit-it school of cricket. And, sure enough, he played a cross-bat heave at the next ball and connected. Two bounces and the ball flew across the boundary and rattled against the wall of the pavilion.

"That's the way to handle spinners, Mack," shouted Frankie. The bowler didn't look very pleased but he kept his cool and the next ball was drilled by Mack straight into the hands of mid-wicket. We were 34 for one.

Azzie looked relaxed right from the start, particularly against the spinner. He plays very late with lots of wrist and it always astonishes me how much power he gets into his shots from apparently little effort. The sweep shot which took us into the fifties was typical of him; it looked almost lazy but the ball raced over the long-leg boundary only seconds after hitting the middle of the bat – pure timing. The fielder had no chance of cutting it off.

Matthew was caught behind off Andy Laycock. He pushed forward and didn't get quite to the pitch. The turning ball took a fine outside edge and the keeper did the rest. Matthew had scored 16 and he got a generous reception as he walked up to the pavilion.

"Carnival cricket," shouted Curley.

"Slogger Rose," yelled Frankie.

That brought Clive to the wicket to join Azzie. For two class batsmen they haven't had as many big partnerships for Glory Gardens as they should have, partly because Clive's always trying to outdo Azzie. He once even tried to stop Azzie getting a fifty by hogging the strike.

But today both looked in a class of their own. Azzie is quick to pick the length, darting into position, playing late, merciless on anything short. Clive is much taller; he loves to get on to the front foot and drive. Like all top left-handers he plays the angles

The spinner was bowling beautifully, getting lots of bounce. He gave both batsmen a real contest – beating them more than once. But Clive and Azzie played him brilliantly, upsetting his rhythm by

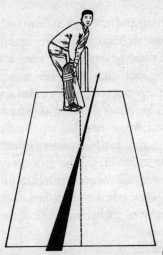

Clive has a second sense about which ball to hit and which one to leave. The right-arm bowler's normal delivery will cut across him. So, if it pitches on off-stump, it will miss the wicket easily. That means Clive can either raise his bat and leave it or, if it's a half volley or a long hop, he'll drive or cut it to the boundary.

Here he makes room for the cut shot by stepping back and rocking on to his left foot. His head is still well over the ball and notice how he plays it down into the ground with a turn of the wrists.

going down the pitch and then glancing and sweeping from the crease. It helped too that one of them was left-handed and the other right because the bowlers had to keep adjusting their line.

After a three-over spell that went for a total of 25 runs, Drax Mill brought back their opening bowler and switched their spinner to the other end. The quicky was was down in Jo's book as B. Challoner. Clive and Azzie revelled in the extra pace. Azzie off drove him twice in a row for four; Clive matched him with a lazy pull to the leg-side boundary. The hundred came up in Andy Laycock's last over with Clive sweeping him for two.

But the sky was getting darker and darker. Curley kept pointing to the clouds which were gathering behind the pavilion. "It looks like a big one," he said.

It was almost like night out in the middle when Azzie hooked Challenor off his nose for a huge six that brought up his fifty. Everyone applauded him and Clive rushed down the wicket to give Azzie the high five. But soon all eyes were back on the black clouds building above and two balls later Clive, Azzie and all the Drax Mill fielders were running flat out for the pavilion as a curtain of rain fell across the pitch.

The pavilion had a tin roof and as the rain pounded against it you could hardly hear yourself speak. It fell in a single sheet; looking out from the pavilion was like standing behind a waterfall.

"Well that's it," said Marty. "End of game."

"I shouldn't count on it," said Curley. "It can stop just as quickly as it starts."

"But we can't play in a swimming pool," said Frankie. "I haven't brought my flippers."

"If it stops soon the sun will dry it in an hour," said Curley.

We had scored 133 for two from just 21.4 overs. The way Clive and Azzie were going along a total of 200 plus was well in our sights. I watched the rain and cursed. Frankie loved it, though. It was the first time he had been cool since he'd arrived on the island and he set off for a walk round the pitch. Ohbert followed him and they'd hardly gone a couple of steps before their clothes were clinging to them. They danced off into the distance where the palm trees were swaying in the wind.

Curley was right. After about fifteen minutes the downpour slowed and then stopped. Soon the sun was shining again from a bright, blue sky. A cloud of vapour rose from the pitch and we walked out to investigate the damage.

Frankie and Ohbert, steaming in the sunshine, joined us in the middle. Ohbert was fiddling with his Walkman. "Oh but, it's stopped," he said.

"You're lucky you didn't electrocute yourself," said Azzie.

"I was hoping there'd be a flash from one ear to the other to charge up his brain," said Frankie. "Funny though, it's never stopped when he's worn it in the showers or when he went shark fishing."

After a long conference the umpires decided that we could play again in an hour.

That left us just over an hour's play because it starts to get dark at 6 o'clock in Barbados and ten minutes later it is dark. So the game was shortened to fifteen overs a side. After 15 overs we had scored 67 so Drax Mill's target was 68.

"It's a rip-off," said Marty. All those runs Azzie and Clive scored won't count. It's not fair."

"Do you realise that Matthew was out in the fourteenth over," said Clive peering at the score-book.

"But it was one of his quicker innings," said Frankie sarcastically. He scored at more than a run an over."

Matthew pretended not to listen. He's had plenty of practice of being teased by Frankie, Clive and the others.

"68 runs – that's about 4.5 an over," I said. "We'll have to defend from the first ball." We'd probably be bowling with a wet ball from the start – that wasn't going to help, either.

I tried hard to get everyone keyed up for a win but as the Drax Mill openers walked out Marty and Clive were still whinging about the umpires' decision. "It should have been 20 overs," said Clive. "Then we'd have had a chance."

Ohbert as usual was wandering around in circles like a badly behaved puppy. "Here, deep mid-off," I shouted to him, walking over to the spot where I wanted him to field.

Ohbert looked at me blankly and then he suddenly smiled. "Oh but . . . it's going again," he said and I heard his Walkman buzzing back to life.

"Take it off," I said wearily but Ohbert just nodded to the beat of the music and smiled at me.

Marty bowled to a field of five in and four out. We couldn't afford the boundaries but, with only 4.5 runs needed an over, we'd have to cut out the singles too. He bowled a good tight line just outside off-stump and only two runs came off his first over.

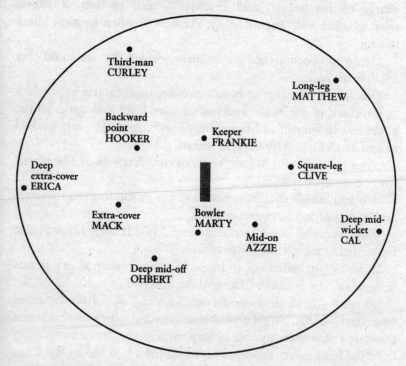

Field placings for Marty's spell

In spite of Cal's success as a surprise opening bowler, this time I gambled on Curley to bowl from the pavilion end and he dropped his third ball short and was hooked for four. Then Cal put down a difficult catch on the cover boundary. The pitch had dried well but the outfield was still quite damp and I think he slipped as he ran in to take it. The bowlers were having to dry the ball on a rag after nearly every delivery and there was still a blustery wind blowing across the pitch which made it difficult for them to get the accuracy we needed.

Curley kept straying to leg and being worked away backward of square. I was forced to bring in an extra fielder on the leg side which meant taking out mid-off and leaving a big inviting hole. That probably gave us our first wicket. The opener drove at Curley aiming for the gap but the ball stopped a bit and flew off a thick edge to Clive at cover point who caught it low to his right in both hands, tumbling over as he took it.

In came Wayne Carew swinging his bat as he walked to the wicket. *Wayne holds the island record for the most sixes in a season.* Victor's words echoed in my head and I dropped another fielder out on the leg-side boundary. Curley's first ball was plonked back over his head for four. He snarled at Wayne who smiled back at him and said, "Wait till I get it in the middle."

That fired Curley up to bowl two beauties which whistled past the batsman's off-stump. But then he pitched a fraction short again and Wayne heaved him in the air over mid-wicket. Azzie was after it. He chased round the boundary with his eyes on the dropping ball. A last despairing dive and he got a hand to it but only enough to deflect it over the rope for another four.

Ohbert dropped a catch driven straight at him off Marty's next over. But he got his chest behind it and stopped the runs. Then I put down a low, miscued drive. "Catch it," shouted Cal and Frankie and it was in my hands and out again before I realised it was a catch. There's nothing I hate more than putting down a chance and I put my head in my hands and walked away.

After eight overs they'd got 41 on the board and they were sailing home. I had to forget about the drop and do something different quickly. But what?

I took Marty and Curley off and brought on Cal and Erica. Wayne Carew immediately hoisted Cal for six, way over Clive's head at deep mid-wicket. He went for the same shot next ball and got completely under it. The ball went straight up in the air. "Mine," shouted Cal as it was still going up. We waited and waited. It seemed as if the ball had gone into orbit. Cal adjusted his position and stood legs apart as it accelerated towards him. He took the catch on one knee and threw the ball up with a huge cry of triumph and relief. It was a big moment in the game and we all knew it.

Erica was straight into her normal tight line and length but at the end of her over they needed only 17 off five overs. Well though Cal and Erica were bowling, Drax Mill were scoring fast enough to get home with overs to spare.

But Glory Gardens hadn't given up. The opener drove Cal to Mack's left at extra-cover and called for a single. A brilliant throw clattered into the stumps and the non-striker was well out of his ground. A couple more stops by Mack and Clive built up the pressure a little more and when Erica took a one-handed caught and bowled from the first ball of the fourteenth over they still needed eight runs from 11 balls.

Ohbert stopped a certain four by diving to his left and landing on the ball with a little squeak of surprise. Matthew made a brilliant interception with his left boot. At last our fielding was clawing us back into the game. As Cal began the fifteenth over they still needed four to win. I'd half thought of bringing Marty back for the last over but Cal was bowling so well I decided he was our best chance.

His first ball was swung away in the air for two just over Clive's head. The next beat the batsman in the air and just missed the stumps; the third bowled him. With three balls remaining Andy Laycock strode out to the wicket, took a big swing at Cal's first ball and left again with his stumps rearranged. Now everything was happening. Cal was on a hat-trick; they needed two to win and there were two balls remaining. The new batsman dug out a yorker fired in at his leg stump and there was no hat-trick but, more importantly, no run.

I'd brought everyone in for the hat-trick ball. Now they moved out slightly for the last ball of the over. There were five fielders on the one and four a little deeper sweeping to prevent them running two. Cal ran in and stopped. The batsman wasn't ready. He turned and ran again. Just four paces and the ball pitched just outside the off-stump. The batsman flashed. He got an edge and it squirted to Frankie's right. Marty was already chasing after the ball when somehow Frankie took off. Just as the ball seemed to be past him he got a hand to it and it stuck deep in his glove.

"Yes!" shouted Cal triumphantly doing a cartwheel down the pitch. It was an heroic catch, the sort that wins matches. We had won – by just one run.

Frankie threw the ball in the air. "I hope you all noticed that, in addition to that moment of genius, there were no byes," he said calmly.

"An all-time first for Frankie Allen," said Azzie slapping him on the back.

As we were clapped off the ground I noticed Ohbert on the boundary. He seemed to be surrounded by little flickers of light which switched on and off. Ohbert stood transfixed, his mouth wide open. I pointed him out to Curley.

"Fireflies," he said. "We always get them after a storm."

"I hope Ohbert doesn't swallow them," I said.

BATSMAN	RUNS SCORED	HOW OUT	BOWLER	SCORE
1 M. ROSE	1·1·1·4·2·1·2·2·1·1	ct BECKLES	LAYCOCK	16
2 T. McCURDY	2·1·2·2·1·2·1·4	ct CAREW	LAYCOCK	15
3 A. NAZAR	1·4·1·2·1·4·2·1·3·1·4·4·1·1·4 4·3(4)4·1·1·6	NOT	OUT	53
4 C. DA COSTA	4·2·1·2·4·2·2·1·2·2·1·4·1·4· 1·4·1·	NOT	OUT	38
5 C. JOHNSON				
6 E. DAVIES				
7 C. SEBASTIEN				
8 H. KNIGHT				
9 F. ALLEN	AFTER 21·4 OVERS			
10 M. LEAR				
11 P. BENNETT				

INNINGS OF GLORY GARDENS   TOSS WON BY G.G.   WEATHER CLOUDY

FALL OF WICKETS

	1	2	3	4	5	6	7	8	9	10
SCORE	34	59								
BAT NO	2	1								

BYES	2·1·1·2·2		8	TOTAL EXTRAS	11
L BYES	1			TOTAL	133
WIDES	1			FOR	
NO BALLS	1			WKTS	2

SCORE AT A GLANCE

BOWLING ANALYSIS · NO BALL ▲ WIDE

BOWLER	1	2	3	4	5	6	7	8	9	10	11	12	13	OVS	MDS	RUNS	WKT
1 I. BOURDIEU	··1·2 ·1·1	·1· 1·7	·2· 1·2·	·1· 2··	··4 ··	·1·· 121	X							6	0	25	0
2 B. CHALLENOR	·1· ···	·2· 2··	··2	X	·120 144	04· ·1·3	+11 6·							5·4	0	37	0
3 A. LAYCOCK	·4W ·1	··2 ·21	·4·	W	··2 ·4·	X	·2· 2·1							6	1	25	2
4 J. HOLFOLD	··3 ··1	1·4 2·1	·44 ·12	X										3	0	23	0
5 F. GOODMAN	4·· 414													1	0	14	0
6																	
7																	
8																	
9																	

INNINGS OF DRAX MILL COLLEGE · TOSS WON BY G.G. WEATHER Sunny.

BATSMAN	RUNS SCORED	HOW OUT	BOWLER	SCORE
1 T. FARMER	1·1·1·2·2·2·1·2·2·2·1·1	c & b	DAVIES	18
2 R. DYAL	1·4·2·1·2·1·1·1	ct DA COSTA	JOHNSON	13
3 W. CAREW	4·4·4·6	c & b	SEBASTIEN	18
4 J. HOLFORD	1·1·1·2·1	RUN	OUT	6
5 H. BECKLES	2·1	NOT	OUT	3
6 F. GOODMAN	1·1·2	bowled	SEBASTIEN	4
7 A. LAYCOCK		bowled	SEBASTIEN	0
8 W. STODDARD		ct ALLEN	SEBASTIEN	0
9 J. BOURDIEU	GAME REDUCED TO 15			
10 L HEWITT	OVERS. GLORY GARDENS WIN			
11 B. CHALLENOR	ON FASTER SCORING RATE			

FALL OF WICKETS											BYES	—	0	TOTAL EXTRAS	4
	1	2	3	4	5	6	7	8	9	10	L BYES	1·1·1	3	TOTAL	66
SCORE	21	47	58	60	66	66	66				WIDES	1·	1	FOR	
BAT NO	2	3	4	1	6	7	8				NO BALLS			WKTS	7

SCORE AT A GLANCE

BOWLER	BOWLING ANALYSIS · NO BALL · WIDE													OVS	MDS	RUNS	WKT
	1	2	3	4	5	6	7	8	9	10	11	12	13				
1 M. LEAR	··1 1··	·+·2 ··1	2·· 2··1	··2 1·4	✗									4	0	17	0
2 C. JOHNSON	··4 ·21	1·1 1·1	·W4 ··4	··2 2··	✗									4	0	23	1
3 C. SEBASTIEN	·6W ··1	·1· ·112	··· 2··	2·W W·W										4	0	14	4
4 E. DAVIES	··· 2··	·2· ·11	N·1 ·11											3	0	9	1
5																	
6																	
7																	
8																	
9																	

Chapter Thirteen

POST CARD

We've only got two days left in Barbados but they are going to be brilliant. Today we're making costumes for the Carnival party after our game against Griffiths Hall. Frankie's going as Dracula and Tylan's making a shark. I don't know what I'm going to be yet maybe Robin Hood. Yesterday we won again. Azzie got 53 not out. Just off to the beach. How's the weather in England? Freezing, I hope!

Harry

We had a six-a-side game on the beach before lunch and both Jacky and Tylan claimed that they had passed their fitness tests. Jacky bowled well; his finger didn't seem to be giving him any trouble at all. I was more concerned about Tylan who was still limping slightly. But it was difficult to get any sense out of him. All he wanted to talk about was his brilliant fishing trip and the giant tuna he'd caught and the even bigger one that got away. There wasn't much doubt, though, that he wanted to play in the Griffiths Hall game and it looked more and more likely that we would have the full squad of 12 players to choose from for the first time since our opening match.

After lunch we started making our outfits for the Carnival. Clive's aunt brought along several sacks full of material and paper and old clothes and hats for us to use. Kiddo wasn't going to be left out of the fun. He'd decided to go as a pirate and Frankie found him standing in front of the mirror with a patch over his eye, talking to himself.

"Come and see Captain Kiddo," whispered Frankie and we all crept up on him.

"Right there, Jim, lad," said Kiddo in a sort of strangled voice. "Yo ho ho and a bottle of rum." He went bright red when he saw us watching him.

"Perhaps Ohbert could go as your parrot and sit on your shoulder," suggested Tylan.

"Where *is* Ohbert?" asked Azzie who was making a huge, brightly coloured mask of an elephant's head.

"I last saw him in our room going through the first-aid box," said Frankie.

"He's not hurt himself, has he?" I asked.

"He doesn't seem any worse than usual," replied Frankie. Frankie's Dracula costume was heavily smeared in tomato sauce which was cooking in the sun and beginning to smell like a pizza. His cloak was made from two black plastic rubbish bags and he'd cut the teeth out of a margarine box; they looked rather strange with yellow and red writing across them.

I'd changed my mind about Robin Hood, partly because Marty had had the same idea but mainly because Cal found two bowler hats in Clive's aunt's sacks and he persuaded me to go as half of Thomson and Thompson from Tintin. I think I was Thompson. Jo had brought "The Red Sea Sharks" on holiday with her and we copied from the pictures. The hardest bits were the moustaches and the round noses.

By the end of the afternoon we all had made a costume of one sort or another. Clive was Superman; Matthew, W.G. Grace – he looked good but I didn't envy him wearing all that padding. Erica was a very grand Queen Elizabeth I. But the best two, everyone agreed, were Jo who had made a brilliant Pocahontas costume and Tylan's shark. Tylan's head emerged from the mouth of the shark and it looked as if he had been swallowed by it feet first. Ty's easily the best artist at school and the shark's head and teeth looked quite realistic. Ohbert nearly jumped into the pool with fright when he first caught sight of it. Poor Ohbert was probably still having nightmares about his fishing expedition.

"Where have you been, Ohbert?" asked Jo.

"I like your Carnival costume," said Frankie looking at Ohbert's green shorts and a tee-shirt which went from pink to bright red. "Is it a chaffinch? Perhaps you should paint your nose yellow."

"Oh but, no it's not," said Ohbert crossly, still eyeing the shark suspiciously.

"Then what are you going to be, Ohbert?" asked Erica. But no-one could get him to say what or where his costume was or what he'd been doing all afternoon. He pounced on a pair of thick white tights in the bundle of clothes and scuttled back to his chalet.

———————— • ————————

We arrived early at Griffiths Hall School for the big match. Flags were flying all round the ground and there was a temporary wooden stand on one side of the pavilion which shone brilliant white in the sun.

Henderson introduced us to his headteacher who told Kiddo that he had seen him play once in England when he got 49 against Middlesex and was out trying to reach his fifty with a six.

"I remember it well," said Kiddo. "I was clean bowled. It was my highest score at Lord's." Frankie made a siren noise which is his boring-Kiddo-story warning and we all took his cue and escaped leaving the head listening politely to Kiddo's blow-by-blow account of his cameo innings.

The ground was starting to fill up as the whole school finished their lessons and poured on to the cricket ground. This was going to be the biggest crowd we'd ever played in front of and, apart from Jo, Kiddo and Clive's aunt, they'd all be shouting for Griffiths Hall.

I had left the final selection of the team to the last minute to be sure that Tylan's and Jacky's injuries weren't playing up. But now was the moment of truth. The Selection Committee, Marty, Jo and I, gathered to decide who was going to be the unlucky player to miss the game.

Marty wanted to drop Ohbert and I suppose he was the logical choice because, let's face it, in spite of everything, he still can't play cricket.

"There'll be a riot if Ohbert doesn't play," said Jo. "Loads of his fans are coming and Victor says everyone at Griffiths Hall is talking about his innings at Yorkshire. If he wants to play I think someone else should stand down." Jo always sticks up for Ohbert and this time she had a point.

It's always the same with the Glory Gardens' Selection Committee. Jo and Marty usually disagree and I'm left in the middle. "I think anyone who has missed a match should definitely play," I said.

"So Tylan, Jacky and Frankie are in," said Jo writing down their names.

"And we can't afford to drop a bowler," said Marty. "We've got six but two of them are half injured. Tylan still looks a bit wobbly."

"Then it will have to be one of the weaker batters. Mack or Matthew," said Jo.

"I still don't see why we can't drop Ohbert," said Marty sullenly.

"Well we just can't, can we Hooker?"

"I'm not sure," I said bravely standing up to Jo. "But I've got an idea." Marty and Jo looked at me. "We could say that we can't make up our minds and then have a competition for twelfth man between Ohbert, Matthew and Mack."

"Yeah. How about an intelligence test?" said Marty. "Ohbert's bound to come last in that."

"No," said Jo firmly. "We'll just draw straws."

And that's what we did. Jo took three drinking straws and cut them off at different lengths and then she held one end of them in her fist and Matthew, Mack and Ohbert each had to choose a straw.

"OK then, the one who picks the shortest straw will be twelfth man," said Jo.

It was some time before Ohbert understood what he had to do and then he took ages to choose his straw. "If you don't make up your mind soon, Ohbert, I'm going to strangle you," said Jo sharply.

Ohbert quickly grabbed a straw. It was the longest one. Mack drew the shortest. He smiled. "Come on, Ohbert, I'll give you some fielding practice. You're going to need it," he said trying to hide his disappointment.

So, in the end, this was the side we put out against Griffiths Hall School:

Matthew Rose
Cal Sebastien
Azzie Nazar
Clive da Costa
Erica Davies
Hooker Knight
Frankie Allen
Tylan Vellacott
Jacky Gunn
Marty Lear
Ohbert Bennett

Mack McCurdy (12th man)

This time I was going to bat at number six as usual; I hadn't batted or bowled in our win at Drax Mill. I was worried about leaving Mack out. He's not just our best fielder, he's also brilliant at motivating everyone by his example. So I decided to give a short team talk about our fielding and catching. It wasn't easy since I'd been the last one to drop a catch.

"It's going to be like a replay of the World Cup," I began. "We know they've got some brilliant players and they're going to try even harder in front of their own crowd. So we can't afford to give away runs in the field or drop any catches. We've got to concentrate on our . . ." I stopped as Frankie threw a cricket ball straight at my chest and it bounced off my left thumb as I tried to protect myself.

"Sorry. I was trying to remember when you last caught one," said Frankie, grinning broadly.

Marty looked accusingly at Frankie. "I don't know how you've got the nerve, Frankie. If I added up all the catches you'd dropped off my bowling I'd have twice as many wickets."

"What we need is an incentive," said Cal. "For instance, you get 50p for a catch and a 50p fine if you drop one."

"Frankie may as well pay up his fiver, now," said Marty.

In the end we agreed – because all our money was in Barbadian dollars – that we'd each be paid $2 for a catch and $1 for a good bit of fielding but $2 would be deducted for a dropped catch and $1 for a misfield – there are about three Barbadian dollars to £1. Mack was put in charge of bonuses and fines for the game. It was up to him to decide when a catch went down. "Do I count the one you've just dropped?" he asked me.

So I got the result I wanted without having to lecture anyone. You don't get anywhere by being too serious with Glory Gardens. I once asked Kiddo what were the most important things to remember when you're captaining a side; he said there were three: "Don't play for yourself or everyone else will do the same; keep two overs ahead of the game and keep a sense of humour."

Sometimes, with players like Frankie and Ohbert in the team, keeping a sense of humour is a struggle. But if you play for Glory Gardens the most important thing is to enjoy yourself. That means winning, too – because there's nothing more enjoyable than a good win.

Henderson and I were applauded and cheered by the whole school as we walked out to toss up. He told me he was going to win the toss and put us in. And he did. On the way back I told him we were going to win the game. He shook his head and smiled. "They'll lynch us if we lose," he said looking around at the crowd. "So you can wave goodbye to the Carnival Shield."

"The what?"

"The Carnival Shield. It's what we're playing for. The head decided there had to be a trophy to mark this historic game. You'll see it in the pavilion."

"And it's on its way to England."

Henderson shook his head. "Richard Wallace has put on a yard of pace since last year," he said.

Chapter Fourteen

"**A**re you Ohbert?" a small boy asked Matthew as he and Cal made their way down the pavilion steps.

"Certainly not," said Matthew crossly.

The two of them couldn't have looked more different as they walked out to the middle: Cal, tall and athletic, and Matthew, short and slightly round shouldered, wrapped in his helmet and arm guard. They'd both faced Richard Wallace and Thompson Gale before, so they knew exactly what to expect. And they almost appeared to be looking forward to it.

Richard Wallace is the quickest bowler I've ever faced – and that includes Vincent Haynes of Wanderers Bay. Thompson Gale is not much slower and what he lacks in pace he makes up for in guile. Thompson's slower ball is just like a leg break and even Azzie says you can't pick it until after if has left his hand.

Richard's first delivery was, predictably, a bouncer. The school cheered and Matthew ducked under it. After leaving three more short, fast balls, he eventually got the score-board moving with a leg glance for two played deftly off his hips. This time the Glory Gardens supporters cheered. It sounded rather pathetic compared with the full-throated roar of the whole school.

Cal's first scoring shot was a boundary. He pulled Thompson square the moment he dropped short. But the bowlers had plenty to shout about, too. The ground resounded with oohs and aahs as time and again they went past the bat and in the fourth over of the innings, Thompson had an enormous shout for lbw against Matthew turned down.

In Richard's next over there was an even bigger appeal as an inswinging yorker ripped into Matthew's pads; this time the umpire was in no doubt and the dreaded finger shot up.

Azzie scurried out to the wicket and didn't hang about getting his eye in. The second ball he received was hooked right off the middle for four.

"Is *he* Ohbert, then?" the same small boy leaned over and asked Matthew who was taking off his pads.

"No," snapped Matthew, "Ohbert bats eleven."

"But I thought he was your star batsman," said the boy.

"He is. You've never seen anything like him," said Frankie. The boy looked puzzled.

After five overs we were 18 for one. Cal still appeared to be slightly out of touch and he was scratching about a bit but Azzie was in amazing form. He glanced Thompson for two and then drove him square to the cover-point boundary. In Richard's next over he got another short-pitched delivery and hooked hard and high for four. We were still applauding when we heard the appeal from the keeper.

"What's going on?" said Tylan.

"One of the bails is on the ground," said Jo. "He must have hit his wicket."

"The umpire's given him out," said Erica.

It wasn't until Azzie got back to the pavilion that we found out exactly what had happened. "It's my bat," he said, holding it out for us to see. A piece of the toe of the bat was missing. "It broke off as I played the shot," continued Azzie. "And it hit me on the head and dropped on the wicket. The umpire said it was the unluckiest thing he'd ever seen on a cricket field but he had to give me out."

"Hit wicket, then," said Jo, entering it in her score-book.

"You've had that bat longer than I've known you," said Frankie. "You should have used one of the new ones."

"But I like it," said Azzie sadly. "At least, I used to."

Clive took guard and ducked under a welcoming bouncer from Richard. He edged the next ball through the slips.

After eight overs the speed twins were taken off and replaced by

Victor and Vaughan Tossell. Victor bowls little cutters but he can get the ball to go both ways. Vaughan's a handy leg spinner; he comes in off only a couple of paces but he's surprisingly quick and he's got a lethal top spinner which really skids through off the pitch.

The wrist spinner's top spinner is an important ball in the armory. The ball is spun towards the batsman and when it hits the pitch it gains pace and hurries on. Notice how the bowler's hand rotates over the top of the ball – the back of the hand will finish up facing the batsman.

Cal began to look more relaxed and Clive played a series of beautiful shots against the spinner. He brought up the fifty with the best of the lot – a silky off drive off the front foot which simply flew between mid-off and the bowler and left them both gasping in stunned admiration.

Next over Cal swept Vaughan for another four but then he attempted to repeat the shot and missed. The ball flicked off his pads down the leg side and deflected off Henderson's pads. Cal looked over his shoulder and, without waiting for Clive's call, set off for the leg-bye.

"No!" screamed Clive. The ball had only run a couple of yards away from the wicket-keeper and he ripped off a glove and was on it in a flash. As Cal turned Henderson flicked the ball backwards and hit the stumps.

"Is that stumped or run out?" asked Matthew.

"Who cares? Either way it's out," said Frankie.

Jo looked at her brother sadly and wrote 'RUN OUT 20' against Cal's name.

Meanwhile, Clive seemed indestructible. He loves to drive and this was such a true, fast pitch that he could drive on the up, even against Victor Eddy. Yet another four went screaming past extra-cover and the home crowd applauded generously. The next ball was pitched up and Clive hit it even harder straight back at the bowler. The ball never rose more than six inches off the ground and it was travelling at the speed of light. We were all looking towards the boundary and I think Victor was trying to get out of the way when the ball hit his boot. It ricocheted sharply off to the right and just carried to Gary Lomas at mid-off. He dived forward and took the catch.

"I don't believe it," said Azzie. "Caught off the bowler's foot."

"That's two of the unluckiest dismissals I've seen in thirty years of playing cricket," pronounced Kiddo.

"Just watch out, Hooker," said Frankie seeing me ready to go out to the wicket. "Everyone's getting out in weird ways today. Watch out for 'handled the ball' or 'obstructing the fielders'."

I joined Erica in the middle. The fall of two quick wickets meant that we had to start again and rebuild the innings. The score-board looked healthy enough on 69. But with four wickets down and half the overs gone we needed to keep the momentum going without losing any more wickets.

Henderson decided the time had come to bring Thompson back

into the attack and I faced up to him. I tried hard to get on to the front foot but it wasn't easy with the pace and bounce he was generating. Twice the ball flashed past my groping outside edge. Then I got a shortish delivery and I went to pull it on the leg side; it was on me quicker than I expected and I finished up flat-batting it for four straight back past the bowler. Thompson glared down the wicket at me, hands on hips. I then got two toe-flattening yorkers and a very fast bouncer. I was happy still to be there at the end of the over.

The spectators were now really gripped by the game. As Thompson came on for his last over there was lots of advice for Henderson about his field placing.

"Give me a sweeper behind square-leg, Hendo. He likes to hit on the on side," shouted one of the older boys.

"Mid-on is too deep. He's in no-man's land," bellowed another.

Thompson bowled me his slower ball and I picked it and hit it back over his head for two.

I tried to remember what Kiddo had told me about my batting. "You've been a bit out of touch so far on tour," he'd told me. "It happens to all of us now and again. The best way to get it back is to limit your stroke play at the beginning of your innings. Try and play straight and hit the ball in the 'V'." That's not easy for a natural leg-side batsman but I tried to keep a straight ball.

Thompson had brought in an extra slip, leaving a big space at mid-on. He bowled to me on off-stump and I leaned into it and drove straight through the gap. I didn't follow through and the ball didn't quite make it to the boundary but we ran three. Kiddo was right; I was already beginning to feel the timing coming back.

Thompson finished his six-over spell and Henderson replaced him with Richard Wallace. I knew he had only two overs left – but what should I do, defend or go on the attack? We had ten overs to go and I estimated we needed another 70 runs.

Richard's first ball went past my off-stump as my bat was still coming down. He hadn't lost any of his pace. The next was up in my ribs and I pushed it down the leg side off the top of my bat for two. The third was short and wide of the off-stump and I gave it everything. The ball shot off a thick outside edge and easily beat the wide third-man fielder to the boundary rope.

Erica came down the pitch to have a word with me. "Don't get carried away," she said. "That's six off the over. Remember one of us needs to be out here at the end."

She was right. I needed to calm down a bit. I left the next two balls outside the off-stump and I was half expecting the famous Wallace yorker which he bowled with his last ball and I blocked it dead in the crease.

Erica took four off the next Griffiths Hall over and, all too soon, I was facing Richard Wallace again. A bouncer screamed past my throat as I jerked back to get out of its way. It slapped into the keeper's gloves and Richard gave me a big grin and turned to continue the assault. A huge cheer ran round the ground – there was no doubt that Richard was the star of the school team.

The cheering started again as he ran in to bowl the next ball. I managed to work it down to long-leg for a single which meant Erica had to face Richard for the first time. He bowled a little too straight and she flicked him away on the leg side with such perfect timing that the ball beat the two chasing fielders to the boundary. Richard came in again. The fastest delivery he'd bowled all day pitched on Erica's off-stump and left her. She was good enough to get the faintest touch on it and the ball melted into Henderson's gloves. Erica and I had put on 34 together. The score was now 97 for five.

A moment later my disappointment at the fall of Erica's wicket turned to horror as I saw the next batsman coming out to join me. It couldn't be . . . but it was. I couldn't believe my eyes. But sure enough there, hidden under Matthew's helmet, was Ohbert meandering out to the middle. The word was passed round the ground that the 'star' of Glory Gardens' batting had arrived. The whole crowd was suddenly buzzing with anticipation. A chant of 'Ohbert, Ohbert' rose from the far corner of the ground.

"Whatever are *you* doing here?" I hissed at Ohbert as he strolled past me.

"Oh but, Hooker. Frankie told me to get my pads on and then, when Erica was out, he'd disappeared . . ."

"And so you had to come in because no-one else was padded up."
I was beginning to understand.

Ohbert nodded.

"I might have known that Frankie had something to do with it,"
I said. I was so angry that I forgot to give Ohbert any instructions
and he waddled down to the striker's end to face the final two balls
of the fastest young bowler in Barbados. At least it was his last
over.

As Richard ran in the roar of the crowd grew louder and louder.
Just as he was about to bowl Ohbert stepped back from the crease
and pulled off his helmet. Richard came to a crunching halt and
glared at Ohbert who was waving frantically at a fly or a mosquito.
He grinned at Richard. "Oh but, sorry. I think I'm ready now."

At last Richard ran in again and bowled a wild, short delivery
way down the leg side which made Ohbert's forward defensive
played nearly two yards away from the ball look even more peculiar
than usual. The umpire signalled a wide.

Ripples of laughter ran through the crowd and Richard
scratched his head. His next ball was a straight yorker and Ohbert
saw it at the last moment and turned his back on it. Somehow the
ball hit the toe of his bat and flew wide of the keeper to the
unguarded fine-leg boundary. The four brought up our hundred but
it was Ohbert not the hundred that the crowd cheered.

One more ball of Richard's over – I held my breath. It was short
and rising over middle stump when Ohbert gloved it to first slip. It
was a straightforward catch but Henderson dived in front of the
slip fielder and pushed it round him. We ran two – Ohbert nearly
ran himself out turning for the third but the whole crowd screamed
'No' and he stopped and put his bat back in the crease just in time.

Richard's final over had cost us Erica's wicket but it had also
gone for 12 runs. My main worry now was to keep Ohbert away
from the bowling as much as possible. Unfortunately the crowd
didn't agree with me. There were loud boos when I refused singles
off the first two balls of the next over. I swung the third away for
four over square-leg and then took a single off the next ball. That

left just two for Ohbert to face.

The new bowler at the school end was bowling medium-pace leg-cutters, not that it mattered to Ohbert who greeted his next ball with another forward defensive and survived a very loud appeal for lbw from virtually the whole team. Ohbert looked faintly surprised at all the shouting.

The last ball of the over was on middle stump and Ohbert ran straight down the pitch at it – the ball emerged from a flurry of bat and pad and Ohbert kept running in my direction. I thought for a split second of keeping my bat in the crease and running him out. But then I found myself haring down the pitch with the odds on being run out myself. Fortunately the direct throw missed the stumps and I slid my bat in just before Henderson had the bails off.

I cursed Frankie and tried to attract Ohbert's attention but he'd gone for a walk over in the direction of the square-leg umpire and he was talking to himself excitedly. Henderson brought back Vaughan Tossell, the leg spinner, to bowl at Ohbert. Ohbert watched in amazement as three balls pitched on middle stump and spun past his off-stump. He didn't even attempt to play a shot to any of them. After the third ball he walked down the wicket and tapped the pitch with his bat. The crowd thought that was a great joke and roared with laughter.

Then Vaughan bowled a slower ball and Ohbert tried his other shot, the 'ohfensive' stroke. He was through with his shot long before the ball arrived so he had another go at it – a sort of backhand with the reverse of the bat. He connected just as the ball was looping into the stumps and sent the keeper the wrong way. Vaughan groaned in disbelief as he watched the ball deflect away for three runs. That brought Ohbert to double figures and I could hear Frankie's voice above the cheers of the crowd: "Hooker, he's outscoring you. Get going or get out."

I began to feel as if I was living through a nightmare but I tried to keep my concentration going. I swept Vaughan against the spin for two and then I drove him into the covers for a single to keep the strike.

Somehow or other we'd reached 116 for five and six overs of the innings remained. The next over was not a good one. I was looking for the boundaries and I kept hitting it straight to the fielders. I couldn't even get a single off the last ball.

So, once more, Ohbert faced up to the spin of Vaughan Tossell. Vaughan bowled him a lowish full toss and as Ohbert stepped back to play it he got his legs tangled up with his bat and he fell back and sat on his stumps at exactly the same moment as the ball hit his foot and cannoned into the middle peg. The crowd groaned and Ohbert stood up and stared at the wreckage he'd made of the wicket.

"Am I out?"

Take your pick, I thought – hit wicket, lbw and bowled – but definitely out. There was a standing ovation for him as he walked back to the pavilion waving his bat at the crowd.

Frankie tried to make his way to the wicket without catching my eye but I cornered him. "So what's the big idea?" I said.

"What?"

"Sending Ohbert in at seven?"

"Yes, er, I'm sorry about that. I went to the loo at the wrong time," Frankie grinned at me.

I sighed. "We want quick runs . . . but don't go mad. Play straight," I said.

Frankie winked and shuffled off to the other end to face Vaughan. He didn't have a clue about the first two balls which whizzed by outside his off-stump. Then he got one which was a bit overpitched and back it went over Vaughan's head for four.

The field was now set well out and I decided to milk the singles for an over or two. The problem was that Frankie's not the ideal partner for quick singles. After we'd run a few of them he came lumbering, red-faced, down the wicket to complain to me. "Just because you can run like a rabbit doesn't mean you can expect everyone else to be as quick," he panted.

"If you don't want to run you'd better knock some boundaries," I said.

"You bet," said Frankie wiping his brow. In desperation he then carted the next ball high over mid-wicket for another four.

It wasn't just that Frankie was getting slower and slower on the singles; his calling wasn't much help either. He drove off the edge straight to cover point.

"Yes," he shouted – then he saw the fielder. "No, wait, yes, no. Maybe."

I was doing a little backwards and forwards dance at the other end and as the fielder fumbled and Frankie started to run without a call I shouted, "No!" as loudly as I could. Frankie turned and his feet went straight up in the air. Before he could scramble up the throw was in and Henderson had executed the run out. Frankie glared at me accusingly before he walked off. What a nerve!

With two overs to go we were on 136. I told Tylan that I was going to go for it and that he should push the singles and give me as much strike as he could. I stood back and cut wide of cover point for four. I followed that with a sweetly-timed straight drive which was brilliantly stopped on the boundary but we ran a couple.

As the last over began we had 145 for seven on the board and Henderson was forced to introduce a new bowler, Cardinal Williams, to finish off the innings. Cardinal's more of a batter than a bowler and he gave me a juicy long hop first ball which I swung away for four. I missed the next completely – probably trying to hit it too hard. I had already made up my mind to go down the pitch to the next and he bowled it just on the right spot for me. I drove it high over the bowler's head and I knew as I hit it that it was going a long way. The umpire turned and watched it and then raised both arms. Six!

The crowd cheered and whistled and when the applause died down for the six I heard Jo shout, "That's his fifty," and the clapping and cheering started all over again.

We finished the innings on 159 for seven. I got 54. Frankie slapped me on the back as I walked up the pavilion steps. "Of course, I'd have got fifty too if you hadn't run me out," he said.

INNINGS OF GLORY GARDENS .... TOSS WON BY G.H.S. WEATHER HOT

BATSMAN	RUNS SCORED	HOW OUT	BOWLER	SCORE
1 M. ROSE	2·1	lbw	WALLACE	3
2 C. SEBASTIEN	4·2·1·1·1·1·2·1·2·1·4	RUN	OUT	20
3 A. NAZAR	4·2·4	hit wkt.	WALLACE	10
4 C. DA COSTA	1·2·1·1·2·2·4·1·2·4·4	Ct LOMAS	EDDY	24
5 E. DAVIES	2·2·2·2·2·2·4	Ct SPRINGER	WALLACE	16
6 H. KNIGHT	1·4·2·3·1·2·4·1·4·1·2·1·2·1·1 1·1·1·4·(37)·2·1·1·4·6·(51)·1·2	NOT	OUT	54
7 P. BENNETT	4·2·1·3	hit wkt.	TOSSELL	10
8 F. ALLEN	4·2·1·4·1	RUN	OUT	12
9 T. VELLACOTT	1·1	NOT	OUT	2
10 J. GUNN				
11 M. LEAR				

FALL OF WICKETS											BYES	2·		2	TOTAL EXTRAS	8
	1	2	3	4	5	6	7	8	9	10	L BYES	1·1·1		3	TOTAL FOR	159
SCORE	14	26	59	63	97	118	136				WIDES	1·1·1		3		
BAT NO	1	3	2	4	5	7	8				NO BALLS				WKTS	7

SCORE AT A GLANCE

BOWLING ANALYSIS · NO BALL + WIDE																	
BOWLER	1	2	3	4	5	6	7	8	9	10	11	12	13	OVS	MDS	RUNS	WKT
1 R. WALLACE	·2··	·2·	w·4·1			·24	·14							6	0	29	3
2 T. GALE	·1	M	·1		·4	·2								6	1	24	0
3 V. EDDY	+··	2·1		4W2	·2·	2·2								6	0	24	1
4 V. TOSSELL	1·2	·2·	·4		···	W··	·1							6	0	34	1
5 I. CUMMINS	·2	·4	···2	111	·42									5	0	29	0
6 C. WILLIAMS	4·6													1	0	14	0
7																	
8																	
9																	

Chapter Fifteen

The biggest cheer of the day greeted Ohbert when he emerged to field. He appeared a little later than the rest of us because we'd forgotten to tell him it was time to start and he was still sitting in the changing room listening to his Walkman when Azzie went back to fetch him.

I went for an attacking field with two slips and a gully for Marty and he roared in to bowl to Victor who was opening the batting with the left-hander, Gary Lomas. Marty was immediately into top gear and he gave both batsmen a bit of the 'hurry up' in his first over.

At the end of it he marched off to long-leg and I threw the ball to Jacky. Jacky hadn't bowled in a proper game since last summer and I was worried about how he would respond. If he was nervous he certainly didn't show it.

"I'll have an extra fielder on the off, please, Hooker," he said. "I won't be bowling any down the leg side." Jacky's got a good memory for the batsmen he's played against. Victor loves to drive, even early on in his innings and Jacky set a field to tempt him to do just that.

His first ball couldn't have been worse if it had come out of a nightmare. It was a no ball, short and down the leg side. Victor played it down backward of square and it ran away to the boundary. Jacky rolled up his sleeves and walked back to his mark without looking at anyone. The next delivery, and the five that followed it, pitched bang on off-stump. The last moved away and took an edge of Victor's bat and Frankie fumbled and gave away a

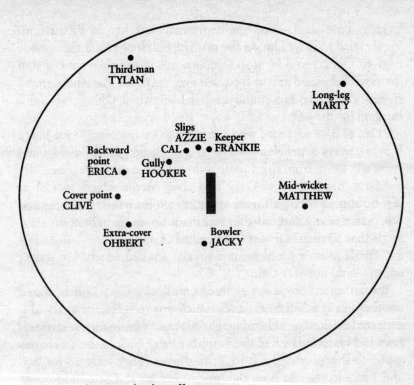

Jacky attacks outside the off-stump

bye. It wasn't a catch because it bounced just in front of him.

"First bye of the match," said Cal with an accusing look at our keeper. That's $1." He waved to Mack on the boundary who signalled that he'd spotted the misfield.

"Did you see it swing?" said Frankie. "It was wicked – just when I had it in the gloves."

"It might help if you stood a bit closer to the stumps," said Jacky, taking his sleeveless pullover from the umpire. He always wears it, even on the hottest days.

In his next over Marty gave Gary Lomas too much room outside the off-stump and he was cut away for two and four. He was furious with himself and kicked away at his front foot mark on the crease as if he was taking revenge on the pitch.

Jacky continued – bowling his immaculate line to Victor until Victor tried to drive him on the up. The ball looped off the outside edge to Ohbert and he stood underneath it and then took a step forward and waved at it as it passed over his head. The whole crowd sighed and Clive ran round and fielded while Ohbert was still hunting for the ball.

"Can't I have someone who can catch at extra-cover?" said Jacky. It was always a problem where to put Ohbert in the field but I switched Tylan from third-man and wished I'd done it sooner.

Marty nearly yorked Gary and then Victor edged to Cal at second slip and the ball went straight into his hands and bounced out. Azzie nearly succeeded in picking it up on the rebound.

"Is that $2 each? Or just Cal?" asked Frankie.

"That's Mack's problem, not yours," snarled Marty. He wasn't happy – and nor was Cal.

But after two drops it was third time lucky. Gary Lomas aimed another cut at a ball from Jacky which was too close to him and it deflected off his bat at head height to Azzie who made no mistake. Four balls later Jacky had their number three back in the hutch, too – plumb lbw playing back to an in-dipper. They were 18 for two and I decided to rest both the quicks and see if Erica and I could turn the screw even tighter.

After we'd each bowled an over I was starting to wonder if I'd made a mistake.

Neither of us bowled badly but Victor, sensing the pressure was off just a little, began to middle the ball. He was joined by Henderson Springer who's a good bat and who looked in top nick as he drove Erica through the gap in the covers all along the ground for four.

I dropped a slip out to deep mid-on and then posted gully to square-leg as slowly Griffiths Hall picked up from their shaky start and started to push us on the back foot. By the end of the twelfth over the score had soared to 47 and I was racking my brain for a solution. All this wasn't helping me to keep my mind on my bowling, either.

Perhaps I should bring on Tylan or Cal to change the tempo, I was thinking as I ran in to bowl. Crack, the ball was blasted straight back at me by Victor and I just got my left hand down to it to stop a certain four. It rapped me on the hand just under the thumb and a feeling like an electric shock went straight up my arm. The ball bounced out to cover and the batsman ran one.

I looked at my hand. The seam of the ball had left a bright red impression on it and I could hardly move my thumb. Tylan underarmed the ball to me and it bounced off the same spot. I winced and picked it up. I couldn't grip it properly in my bowling hand.

The next few deliveries were agony. A full toss was driven for two. Then I bowled one that slipped out of my hand and flew straight over the batsman's head for a wide. Frankie did well to stop it because it bounced just in front of him.

"First he runs me out, then he tries to knock me out," he complained.

Cal came over for a word. "Are you okay?"

"Fine," I said. "My thumb's a bit sore but it'll pass."

"What about a break and giving me or Tylan a bowl."

"Maybe," I said walking back to my mark. Kiddo says a good captain should be two overs ahead of the game. At the moment I didn't feel I was even one ball ahead; I was losing the script fast. Gary flicked me away for a single on the on side and Victor powered a perfect drive over the top of the covers for another boundary.

With the last ball of my over I decided to risk a slower one. If Victor picked it up there would probably be another four but I had nothing to lose. I ran in fast and put a lot of shoulder into the delivery to fool him. The ball looped down the pitch; at least it was straight and on a length. Victor did pick it but only at the last moment. He was going through with a vicious straight drive and he stuttered in mid shot. The ball flew high off the bat; it was coming back at me, high above my left shoulder. I stuck out my hand and felt the stab of pain. But the ball stuck.

"OWZTHAT," I growled hurling the ball high in the air and for a second forgetting the numbing ache in my hand. I'd removed their most dangerous batsman; now it was time for someone else to bowl. "Next over this end," I said to Tylan.

Erica bowled a tight maiden spoilt only by Frankie letting through three byes.

"If you kept your legs together it would help," said Azzie after scurrying back to pick up the ball.

"I try to," said Frankie, "but when I bend down they sort of come apart."

Tylan was still limping very slightly when he ran up to bowl his first ball. A full toss took Henderson by surprise and he was annoyed with himself for not taking full advantage of a bad ball. Tylan followed that with a wide down the leg side, another down the off side, one on the stumps and a long hop which Henderson dispatched for four. It wasn't a great over and at the end of it Griffiths Hall had scored 68 for three. With half our overs gone I worked out that they now needed about six an over to win. They'd just taken nine off Tylan without trying!

After yet another accurate over from Erica, Tylan returned to the firing line. His limp seemed a little worse and he was bowling flatter than usual and not giving the ball his usual tweak. Henderson is too good a bat to miss out on many loose deliveries and when Tylan again served him up a juicy full toss he hoisted it over long-on for six.

Again nine came off the over and Marty, Cal and Clive were all wheeling their arms over, trying to convince me it was time for a bowling change. I decided to give Tylan one more.

Erica finished her spell with six overs for 22. She hadn't taken a wicket but to go for under four an over when the Bajans were in full flow was a brilliant piece of defensive bowling. She'd kept us in the match.

Tylan versus Henderson again – and it wasn't looking like an even contest when Tylan's second ball bounced over the ropes for another boundary.

"Give it a bit more air and spin it hard," I said to Tylan. "I'll drop out one of the covers to sweep the boundary."

"Okay," said Tylan but he was looking worried. He floated one up outside Henderson's off-stump and took the edge. The ball just cleared cover point and they ran two. A single took Henderson off strike and Tylan bowled another floater to the other batsman, Coventry Phillips. He went for it and the ball flew off a thick edge low and hard to Clive who dived forward and to his left and took a spectacular catch.

"Got him," said Tylan wiping his forehead with relief. "Pity it was the wrong one, though."

"Now get the other one then," I said. "It's lucky for you you took a wicket – if you hadn't you were off."

Tylan smiled. "I thought for a moment I'd lost my touch," he said. "But once you've got it, you don't lose it."

There were eleven overs left. It was time to bring back Jacky or Marty. I went for Jacky because he'd been amongst the wickets already and Tylan was bowling from Marty's end. So now we had both the invalids bowling.

Jacky hit the spot again with his first ball and even Henderson had some trouble getting him away. The new batsman, Vaughan Tossell, edged him inches short of Frankie and scampered a single while Frankie looked for the ball which had dropped just behind him.

Tylan, his confidence restored, bowled his best over yet. But the luck seemed to have deserted him. Three times he went past the outside edge of Vaughan's flailing bat. Then Frankie dropped him and followed that by letting through two more byes to take Griffiths Hall to 99. Off the first ball of Jacky's next over Frankie gifted them their 100 with yet another bye.

"What's the matter with you today, fatman?" asked Cal. "Get your big body behind it."

"I can't see how they're getting through," said Frankie taking a close look at his gloves.

"It reminds me of an elephant trying to pick up a pea," said Tylan.

A flowing cover drive from Henderson gave him yet another boundary and – though he was beaten outside the off-stump by a quicker delivery from Jacky – he was still looking ominously good. If he was there at the close, we'd lose – there was absolutely no doubt about that.

Henderson late-cut Jacky for another two and as Jacky walked back to his mark I saw his left hand stretch up and scratch the top of his head and then the side of his nose. I looked at Frankie who winked. He'd seen the signal. It meant Jacky was going to bowl his slower ball. Every member of the team knows Jacky's special signal and they were all ready.

As Jacky ran in Frankie crept quietly up to the stumps. Over came the bowler's arm and Henderson was forward driving outside the off-stump. The blade of his bat flashed, but the ball carried on. Frankie took it outside the off-stump and – "OWZTHAT!" – he had the bails off before Henderson could turn. Henderson nearly jumped out of his skin to see Frankie grinning at him from over the stumps and, as the square-leg umpire slowly raised his finger, he gave Vaughan an angry look and walked off.

"What have I done?" Vaughan asked me.

"Didn't you know you can tell the umpire to stop the bowler if you see a fielder moving?" I asked.

"Well, er, sort of . . ." said Vaughan uncertainly.

Frankie takes the ball outside the off-stump but notice that his weight is still on his left leg so that he can quickly flick off the bails and make the stumpimg.

"That includes the wicket-keeper," I said.

"Oh dear," said Vaughan.

"And he was on 49," said Jacky.

"Oh dear, oh dear," said Vaughan looking more and more worried.

"Maybe you'd better stay out here for a bit," said Cal.

"Yes please," said Vaughan.

By now Thompson Gale had made his way to the wicket. "The captain's not pleased with you, Tosser," he said to Vaughan.

"Oh," said Vaughan, looking at his boots.

"Mind, it's his own fault. He shouldn't have been out of his crease," said Thompson smiling.

Jacky greeted him with a good bouncer which wiped the smile off his face. He only just ducked under at the last moment and he glared at Jacky who stared back defiantly.

106 for five and eight overs to bowl. The run rate had crept up a little but it was still under seven an over – on this pitch that was definitely gettable. I decided not to risk Tylan against Thompson who can hit the ball really hard and I brought Cal on instead.

"Don't go away," I said to Tylan. "We may still need you."

Bash. Thompson signalled his intentions by flat-batting Cal's first ball for four. It flew past Tylan at head height and only bounced once before it reached the boundary.

Thompson missed the next ball completely; then he swept hard down to backward square-leg where Marty made a good stop. The fifth delivery was outside the off-stump and Thompson went for another flat-batted pull. He got a top edge and the ball went high in the air. At first it looked like Frankie's catch but it was going away from him all the time towards third-man. He chased after it head in the air.

Under the ball, half way in from the third-man boundary, was Ohbert. If it had been anyone else I'd have shouted his name and told Frankie to leave it. But Ohbert was never going to catch it – not in a lifetime. So I shouted Frankie's name. Still Ohbert stood there watching the ball which was now dropping towards him like an Ohbert-seeking missile. And still Frankie bore down with his gloves thrust out in front of his red, sweaty face.

The ball reached Ohbert with Frankie only two yards away and closing rapidly. We all held our breath. Ohbert put out two hands to protect himself and parried the ball up in the air and over his head. Frankie put on the brakes but it was too late and he clattered into Ohbert, who also bounced high into the air.

Ohbert landed flat on his back. A fraction of a second later the ball droppedanded for a second time... onto Ohbert's stomach. It sat there for a moment like a cherry on a cake and then it started to roll off. But, just as it was about to drop to the ground Ohbert grabbed it in his left hand.

Frankie was first to his feet. He took the ball from Ohbert and held it high. Then he pulled Ohbert up and, even though Ohbert had caught one of their own players, the cheers and chants rang round the ground.

"Ohbert. OHBERT!"

But Ohbert was too wobbly to take too much notice of the adulation. Being bounced by Frankie and then attacked by a cricket ball had knocked the wind out of him. He couldn't stand up, he could hardly breathe. Frankie half carried him to the pavilion and, to further cheers, Ohbert slumped down next to Jo. Mack trotted on as our substitute fielder and I immediately sent him into the covers and dropped Tylan down to third-man.

Jacky bowled his final over and, with Cal settling in well at the other end, it was time for Marty's last three overs. I'd judged it just right – there were five overs left: three for Marty and two to Cal. Griffiths Hall were now on 124 for six – so they still needed around seven an over.

Seven came from Marty's first three balls with a wide, a snicked four and two behind cover point. Another streaky four off the last ball made me wonder if I should have stuck to the slower bowlers. As if to prove it, Cal pegged them back again with another tight six-ball spell which went for only four. Then Marty responded to the challenge with his next over and suddenly there were just two overs left and they needed 14 to win.

Three singles were worked off Cal's first three balls but singles weren't enough now – Griffiths Hall needed a boundary. Cal was bowling just outside off-stump and I had a 5:4 field with a long-off, a deep extra-cover and wide third-man. Vaughan played a little dab fine of the keeper and they ran two. But then Clive made a brilliant stop on the extra-cover boundary to turn what looked like a four into just a single.

As Marty began his last over they still needed seven to win. I kept the field out for the first couple of balls but when Vaughan took a two off the second ball of the over I brought all the fielders in on the single, except for long-leg, the cover sweeper and deep mid-wicket.

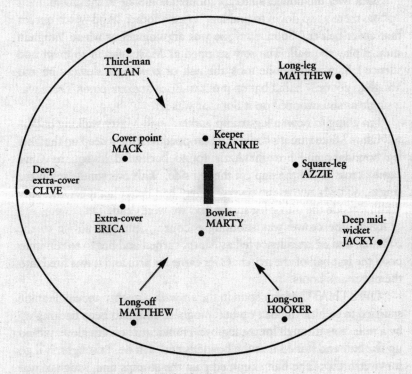

Bringing in the fielders in the last over.

Vaughan leaned back and hit firmly into the covers and was off for another single. But the fielder this time was Mack. He swooped on the ball, swivelled and in one movement threw at the wicket at the striker's end. It was a marvellous throw straight to the base of the off-stump. The whole team went up with the appeal and then we rushed over to congratulate Mack when the umpire gave it. His throw had brought a really dangerous partnership of 44 to an end.

Three balls left and Vaughan was off strike. The new batsman somehow fiddled a very quick delivery from Marty down to fine-leg for a single and Vaughan was again facing. Three to win; two balls remaining. Again I eased the field back, offering him the single but no more.

"Back over the bowler's head," shouted someone in the crowd.

"No there's two down to fine-leg," cried another. "And watch out for that cover fielder." Soon everyone was arguing about where Vaughan should play the ball. The row stopped as Marty ran in to bowl and silence fell. Amazingly he took the risk of bowling a slower one and Vaughan got only half a bat on it out to Erica at extra-cover. There was a single as she swooped on it but that was all.

"I'm going to bowl a leg-stump yorker," said Marty walking back.

"Okay. Make sure it's straight." I dropped Matthew deep on the fine-leg boundary and brought Azzie round backward of square. Clive came across to fill the gap on the leg side. With everyone else on the single and only two in the covers, Marty had better get it on line. Any width outside the off or leg stump and we were dead.

Again, the crowd was shouting encouragment and advice to the batsmen and again, silence fell as Marty turned and began to run in to bowl the last ball of the match. Over came his arm and it was fired into the batsman's boots.

"OWZTHAT!" Marty spun in the air with a mighty appeal. Frankie scurried in to pick the ball up but Vaughan, who had been backing up by a mile, was through for the leg-bye. Frankie tore off his glove, picked up the ball and hurled it at the bowler's end. Oh no, I thought, it'll go for overthrows. The ball skimmed past the stumps and Vaughan was turning for the overthrow when Matthew timed his sliding stop perfectly and held on to the ball.

"No," shouted Vaughan as Matthew threatened to shy at the stumps. And that was it.

The scores stood level on 159. We had tied.

INNINGS OF GRIFFITHS HALL........... TOSS WON BY G.H.S. WEATHER HOT....

BATSMAN	RUNS SCORED	HOW OUT	BOWLER	SCORE
1 V. EDDY	1·4·1·2·1·1·1·2·4·1·1·1·4 》	c & b	KNIGHT	24
2 G. LOMAS	2·4·1 》	ct NAZAR	GUNN	7
3 C. WILLIAMS	2 》	lbw	GUNN	2
4 H. SPRINGER	1·4·4·1·1·3·2·1·4·1·1·6·1·3·1 4·2(40)2·1·4·2	st ALLEN	GUNN	49
5 C. PHILLIPS	2·2·1	ct DA COSTA	VELLACOTT	5
6 V. TOSSELL	1·1·1·2·2·1·2·4·2·4·1·1·2·1·1 1·2·1·2·1	NOT	OUT	33
7 T. GALE	4·2 》	ct BENNETT	SEBASTIEN	6
8 I. CUMMINS	1·1·2·1·1·1·3·1·1·1 》	RUN	OUT	13
9 R. KING	1	NOT	OUT	1
10 S. ADAMS				
11 R. WALLACE				

FALL OF WICKETS											BYES	1·2·2·2·1·1·2·1	12	TOTAL EXTRAS	19
SCORE	16	18	56	92	106	112	156				L BYES	1·1·1	3	TOTAL	159
BAT NO	2	3	1	5	4	7	8				WIDES	1·1·1·	4	FOR	
											NO BALLS			WKTS	7

SCORE AT A GLANCE

BOWLING ANALYSIS · NO BALL · WIDE

BOWLER	1	2	3	4	5	6	7	8	9	10	11	12	13	OVS	MDS	RUNS	WKT
1 M. LEAR	·1 ·1·	1·2 ·4·1	X	4·4·2 ·4·1	·3 ·2·	2· 1·1·				1				6	0	31	0
2 J. GUNN	W	2· 2·1·	·W· 2W	X	·2 ·11	·4· 2W·	12· 2·1	X						6	0	24	3
3 H. KNIGHT	·1 ·11	·2· 4·	·1 ·11	12+1 4W										4	0	20	1
4 E. DAVIES	1· 4·	·4· ·1	·3· M	2· ·11	·3 ·11	X								6	1	22	0
5 T. VELLACOTT	++ 4·2·	·· 6·1·	·42 ·W	X										4	0	24	1
6 C. SEBASTIEN	4·2 ·W1	·2· 1·2·1	1·1· 1··	111 211										4	0	23	1
7																	
8																	
9																	

Chapter Sixteen

Ohbert was none the worse for his crunching, bouncing experience and Frankie and Tylan hoisted him on their shoulders and set off on a lap of honour of the ground. The crowd gave him a hero's reception although one small boy got over excited and threw an orange at him. It hit Tylan on the back of the head and burst.

Ohbert was confused as usual. "Oh but . . . Frankie, why are they shouting at me?"

"Because you're a star, Ohbert. Man of the Match; Personality of the Tour," wheezed Frankie. The extra effort of carrying Ohbert was making him go an alarming shade of beetroot.

"You were outrageous," said Tylan wiping the orange juice out of his hair.

"Was I really?" said Ohbert.

"Some people would fly half way round the world to see a performance like that," said Frankie. "We should have videoed it."

I shook hands with Henderson; we both agreed it had been a great game and that it was a fair result.

"I nearly died in that last over," he said. "I thought you were going to win. I was planning to run away from home."

"Pity you didn't get your fifty," I said. "You batted really well."

"So did you. You make a habit of scoring fifties against us," said Henderson. I remembered well the 69 not out I'd got against Griffiths Hall in the World Cup. It was still my highest score for Glory Gardens.

Mack and Jo were busy sorting out the fielding awards and fines for the game and eventually Mack presented me with a piece of paper:

Fielding Awards

	Good fielding	Misfield	Catches	Drops	Total
Clive	$3		$2		+$5
Azzie	$1		$2		+$3
Erica	$3				+$3
Hooker	$1	$1	$2		+$2
Mack	$2				+$2
Ohbert			$2	$2	–
Matthew	$1	$1			–
Tylan		$1			-$1
Cal				$2	-$2
Frankie	$1	$8		$2	-$9

"That's $9 Francis owes," said Jo. I'll take the money for the fines."

"What are you talking about?" Frankie had just arrived back from his circuit of the ground and he forced his hot, sweaty body to the front to look at the list. "That's not fair! Why have I been fined $8 for misfields?"

"All those byes you let through," said Mack.

"And what about that brilliant stumping? Don't I get anything for that?"

"Yes," said Mack. "$1. And it was just about the only good thing you did."

"But the stumping was worth at least $2 if not $5," stammered Frankie. Jo took no notice of him, though, and sent him off to fetch his money. All the fines were collected and the awards handed out and Matthew had to add $3 from the club funds to make up the difference.

Frankie was still sulking. "How's is it Mack gets $2 when he's supposed to be the judge?" he muttered. "There's something fishy here and I want a fraud investigation." We all ignored him.

"When does the Carnival start?" Cal asked Henderson and just at that moment the school steel band started up in front of the pavilion and as we rushed out to look an extraordinary sight met our eyes.

"Oh no, Captain Kidd's just sailed in," said Frankie. Kiddo was wearing an enormous brimmed hat, a big frilly shirt and extremely tight, red trousers. Two great gold rings dangled from his ears and he had a black beard.

"Well played, my hearties," he said with a broad grin. "Great finish. You bowled and fielded brilliantly."

"You look amazing, Mr Johnstone," said Azzie. "I . . . eh, hardly recognised you."

"Thank you, Asif. But you can call me, Pete – Pete the Pirate."

"I'll stick to Captain Kidd," said Frankie.

"I must get a photo of him for the school notice board," said Cal. No-one is going to believe this."

"That gives me an idea," said Frankie looking around. "But where's Ohbert gone?"

"Signing autographs, I think," said Azzie.

"Well I need him," said Frankie. And he went off to look for him. The rest of us headed for the changing rooms to get into our carnival costumes.

Soon there was a huge procession of the strangest-looking characters winding its way round the school and back to the cricket pavilion where the band was playing. Frankie emerged in his Dracula outfit smelling more and more like a pizza. Galahad and Curley both arrived dressed in bright blue wigs and white dungarees – I don't know who they were supposed to be but they looked amazing. Tylan's shark bobbed in and out of the crowd.

Pete the Pirate led the dancing. "Best tour I've ever been on," he gasped as he stopped for breath and to grab a chicken leg from the barbecue. "And I could tell you about a few of them."

"No thank you, Pete," said Tylan, backing away in case Kiddo started on one of his long stories. "I'd rather walk the plank."

Kiddo shrugged and galloped off for another dance.

"Was he being a pain in the neck?" Frankie asked Tylan baring his Dracula fangs and pretending to sink them into Tylan's throat.

"Where have you been?" asked Tylan. "All this food and no

Frankie. It's not natural."

Frankie grabbed two hamburgers to make up for lost time and took out his Dracula teeth to eat them. "I've been looking for Ohbert but he's gone missing again," he spluttered.

Clive's aunt arrived with a wonderful cake. It had green icing and in the middle was a cricket pitch with wickets and two umpires and a little pavilion. Around the outside she had put the names of all the players from both teams. We each ate the bit with our name on it although Frankie ate Ohbert's too because he still hadn't appeared.

"It's typical of Ohbert. Vanishing just when I wanted him," said Frankie.

"He's probably doing one of his disappearing tricks," said Marty.

"I think that's exactly what he's doing," said Jo pointing to a weird-looking apparition coming towards us. It was covered from head to foot in bandages and a pair of dark glasses were perched on its head. A muffled sound came from somewhere behind the bandages.

"Oh but . . . it's hot in here."

"Ohbert, *what* are you?" said Marty.

"Moby Dick," suggested Frankie.

"Then why's he wearing sunglasses?" asked Cal.

"I know he's a nude sun-bather who has fried in the sun and finished up in hospital," said Tylan.

"Don't be silly," said Jo. "It's obvious. You're the Invisible Man aren't you, Ohbert?"

"Oh but, yes," mumbled Ohbert tripping over a chair and rolling on the ground.

Frankie helped him up and put the sunglasses back on his nose. "I've got a job for you, Ohbert," he said. "Come over here." Frankie dragged and pushed Ohbert along to where a sign was propped up against the side of the pavilion. It read:

HAVE YOUR PHOTO TAKEN
WITH OHBERT
– ONLY $1 –
EVERY PHOTO SIGNED
BY THE AMAZING OHBERT

"I don't suppose it'll matter that you're the Invisible Man . . . but perhaps you could put Matt's helmet on too to show you've been playing cricket," said Frankie. "And some pads and maybe a cricket pullover."

"Oh but . . . I'm hot, Frankie," mumbled the Invisible Man. But Frankie wasn't in the mood to argue and soon Ohbert's fans were lining up to have their picture taken.

The Carnival went on late into the evening and so Glory Gardens' tour of Barbados came to an end. That night we all agreed that, as soon as we got back to England, we'd start saving up for the next one.

POST CARD

Tonight's our last night on Barbados and we've just got back from the Carnival at Griffiths Hall school. It was unbelievable. I hope my photos of Kiddo come out. I took one of him limbo dancing which I'm going to sell to the school magazine. I've got a good one of Ohbert too — on the roof of the pavilion, I don't know how he got up there. Victor was a werewolf and he sent you his love. We tied the game so no one won the Carnival trophy. Henderson says he wants to compete for it again in England next year. I bet you're looking forward to seeing me tomorrow.

Love (ha, ha) Harry

AVERAGES

Batting

	INNS	NOT OUT	RUNS	S/R	H/S	AVERAGE
Azzie	5	1	126	108.6	53*	31.50
Hooker	4	1	87	89.7	54*	29.00
Clive	5	1	99	96.1	38*	24.75
Matthew	5	1	98	40.7	47*	24.50
Cal	4	0	31	52.6	20	7.75
Ohbert	3	1	24	109.1	10	12.00
Frankie	3	0	24	104.3	12	8.00

*denotes 'not out'. Scoring rate (S/R) is based on the average number of runs scored per 100 balls. H/S = highest score. Minimum qualification: 30 runs. Ohbert's and Frankie's averages are included for comparison. Notice who has the higher average.

Highest scores

Hooker	54 not out	v Griffiths Hall
Azzie	53 not out	v Drax Mill College
Azzie	53	v Wanderers Bay

Highest Partnerships

Azzie and Clive	74 v Drax Mill College
Azzie and Matthew	67 v Wanderers Bay
Clive and Matthew	51 v Carlton School

Bowling

	OVERS	MDNS	RUNS	WKTS	S/R	ECON	AVERAGE
Jacky	6	0	24	3	12.0	4.0	8.00
Cal	27	0	103	9	18.0	3.8	11.44
Hooker	17	1	66	5	20.4	3.9	13.20
Erica	23.1	2	63	4	34.8	2.7	15.75
Curley	10	0	49	3	20.0	4.9	16.33
Marty	29	0	135	8	21.8	4.7	16.88
Tylan	13	0	77	4	19.5	5.9	19.25

Strike rate (S/R) is the average number of balls bowled to take each wicket.
Economy rate (ECON) is the average number of runs given away each over.
Minimum qualification 3 wickets.

BEST BOWLING

Cal	4 for 14 v Drax Mill College
Marty	4 for 23 v Yorkshire
Cal	3 for 23 v Yorkshire
Jacky	3 for 24 v Griffiths Hall School

CATCHES

Caught	Dropped	Total
Clive	3	0	+3
Azzie	3	1	+2
Curley	2	0	+2
Mack	2	1	+1
Erica	1	0	+1
Tylan	1	0	+1
Frankie	3	3	–
Cal	2	2	–
Galahad	1	1	–
Hooker	1	1	–
Marty	0	1	-1
Matthew	0	2	-2
Ohbert	1	5	-4

CRICKET COMMENTARY

THE CRICKET PITCH

crease

At each end of the wicket the crease is marked out in white paint like this:

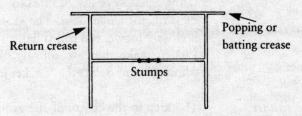

Return crease

Popping or batting crease

Stumps

The batsman is 'in his ground' when his bat or either foot are behind the batting or 'popping' crease. He can only be given out 'stumped' or 'run out' if he is outside the crease. The bowler must not put his front foot down beyond the popping crease when he bowls. And his back foot must be inside the return crease. If he breaks these rules the umpire will call a 'no ball'.

leg side/
off-side

The cricket pitch is divided down the middle. Everything on the side of the batsman's legs in called the 'leg side' or 'on side' and the other side is called the 'off-side'.

Remember, when a left-handed bat is batting, his legs are on the other side. So leg side and off-side switch round.

leg stump

Three stumps and two bails make up each wicket. The 'leg stump' is on the same side as the batsman's legs. Next to it is the 'middle stump' and then the 'off stump'.

off/on side	See **leg side**.
off-stump	See **leg stump**.
pitch	The 'pitch' is the area between the two wickets. It is 22 yards long from wicket to wicket (although it's usually 20 yards for Under 11s and 21 yards for Under 13s). The grass on the pitch is closely mown and rolled flat. Just to make things confusing, sometimes the whole ground is called a 'cricket pitch'.
square	The area in the centre of the ground where the strips are.
strip	Another name for the pitch. They are called strips because there are several pitches side by side on the square. A different one is used for each match.
track	Another name for the pitch or strip.
wicket	'Wicket' means two things, so it can sometimes confuse people. 1 The stumps and the bails at each end of the pitch. The batsman defends his wicket. 2 The pitch itself. So you can talk about a hard wicket or a turning wicket (if it's taking spin).

BATTING

attacking strokes	The attacking strokes in cricket all have names. There are forward strokes (played off the front foot) and backward strokes (played off the back foot).

144

The drawing shows where the different strokes are played around the wicket.

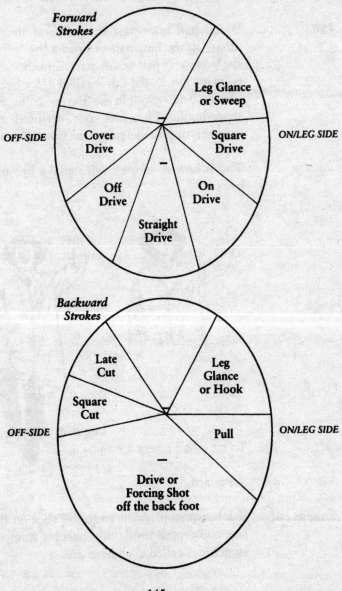

backing up   As the bowler bowls, the non-striking batsman should start moving down the wicket to be ready to run a quick single. This is called 'backing up'.

bye   If the ball goes past the bat and the keeper misses it, the batsman can run a 'bye'. If it hits the batsman's pad or any part of his body (apart from his glove), the run is called a 'leg-bye'. Byes and leg-byes are put in the 'Extras' column in the score-book. They are not credited to the batsman or scored against the bowler's analysis.

This is how an umpire will signal a bye and leg-bye

Bye

Leg-bye

cart   To hit a ball a very long way.

centre   See **guard**.

chinese cut   If a batsman plays an attacking shot on the off side and gets an inside edge past his stumps, it is sometimes called a 'chinese cut'.

cow shot	When the batsman swings across the line of a delivery, aiming towards mid-wicket, it is often called a 'cow shot'.
defensive strokes	There are basically two defensive shots: the 'forward defensive', played off the front foot and the 'backward defensive' played off the back foot.
duck	When a batsman is out before scoring any runs it's called a 'duck'. If he's out first ball for nought it's a 'golden duck'.
flat-back	To hit the ball back down under the wicket with a horizontal rather than straight bat.
gate	If a batsman is bowled after the ball has passed between his bat and pads it is sometimes described as being bowled 'through the gate'.
guard	When you go in to bat the first thing you do is 'take your guard'. You hold your bat sideways in front of the stumps and ask the umpire to give you a guard. He'll show you which way to move the bat until it's in the right position. The usual guards are ' leg stump' (sometimes called 'one leg'); 'middle and leg' ('two leg') and 'centre' or 'middle'.

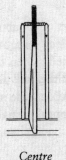 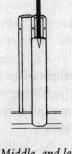 

Centre   Middle and leg   Leg

hit wicket	If the batsman knocks off a bail with his bat or any part of his body when the ball is in play, he is out 'hit wicket'.
innings	This means a batsman's stay at the wicket. 'It was the best *innings* I'd seen Azzie play.' But it can also mean the batting score of the whole team. 'In their first *innings* England scored 360.'
knock	Another word for a batsman's innings.
lbw	Means leg before wicket. In fact a batsman can be given out lbw if the ball hits any part of his body and the umpire thinks it would have hit the stumps. There are two important extra things to remember about lbw: 1 If the ball pitches outside the leg stump and hits the batsman's pads it's not out - even if the ball would have hit the stumps. 2 If the ball pitches outside the off-stump and hits the pad outside the line, it's not out if the batsman is playing a shot. If he's not playing a shot he can still be given out.
leg-bye	See **bye**.
middle/ *middle & leg*	See **guard**.
out	There are six common ways of a batsman being given out in cricket: bowled, caught, lbw, hit wicket, run out and stumped. Then there are a few rare ones like handled the ball and hit the ball twice. When the fielding side thinks the batsman is out they must appeal (usually a shout of 'Owzthat').

148

If the umpire considers the batsman is out, he will signal 'out' like this:

play forward/ back   You play forward by moving your front foot down the wicket towards the bowler as you play the ball. You play back by putting your weight on the back foot and leaning towards the stumps. You play forward to well-pitched-up bowling and back to short-pitched bowling.

rabbit   Poor or tail-end batsman.

run   A run is scored when the batsman hits the ball and runs the length of the pitch. If he fails to reach the popping crease before the ball is thrown in and the bails are taken off, he is 'run out'. Four runs are scored when the ball is hit across the boundary. Six runs are scored when it crosses the boundary without bouncing. This is how the umpire signals 'four':

This is how the umpire signals 'six'.

If the batsman does not put his bat down inside the popping crease at the end of a run before setting off on another run, the umpire will signal 'one short' like this.

A run is then deducted from the total by the scorer.

stance

The stance is the way a batsman stands and holds his bat when he is waiting to receive a delivery. There are many different types of stance. For instance, 'side on', with the shoulder pointing down the wicket; 'square on', with the body turned towards the bowler'; 'bat raised' and so on.

striker	The batsman who is receiving the bowling. The batsman at the other end is called the non-striker.
stumped	If you play and miss and the wicket-keeper knocks a bail off with the ball in his hands, you will be out 'stumped' if you are out of your crease.
ton	A century. One hundred runs scored by a batsman.

BOWLING

arm ball	A variation by the off-spinner (or left-arm spinner) which swings in the air in the opposite direction to the normal spin, ie away from the right-handed batsman in the case of the off-spinner.
beamer	See **full toss**.
block hole	A ball bowled at yorker length is said to pitch in the 'block hole' - ie the place where the batsman marks his guard and rests his bat on the ground when receiving.
bouncer	The bowler pitches the ball very short and bowls it hard into the ground to get extra bounce and surprise the batsman. The ball will often reach the batsman at shoulder height or above. But you have to be a fast bowler to bowl a good bouncer. A slow bouncer is often called a 'long hop' and is easy to pull or cut for four.

chinaman A left-arm bowler who bowls with the normal leg-break action will deliver an off-break to the right-handed batsman. This is called a 'chinaman'.

dot ball A ball from which the batsman does not score a run. It is called this because it goes down as a dot in the score-book.

flipper A variation on the leg-break. It is bowled from beneath the wrist, squeezed out of the fingers, and it skids off the pitch and goes straight through. It shouldn't be attempted by young cricketers because it puts a lot of strain on the wrist and arm ligaments.

full toss A ball which doesn't bounce before reaching the batsman is a full toss. Normally it's easy to score off a full toss, so it's considered a bad ball. A high full toss from a fast bowler is called a 'beamer'. It is very dangerous and should never be bowled deliberately.

googly A 'googly' is an off-break bowled with a leg break action (see leg break) out of the back of the hand like this.

grubber	A ball which hardly bounces - it pitches and shoots through very low, usually after hitting a bump or crack in the pitch. Sometimes also called a shooter.
hat trick	Three wickets from three consecutive balls by one bowler. They don't have to be in the same over ie two wickets from the last two balls of one over and one from the first of the next
half-volley	See **length**
leg break/ off-break	The 'leg break' is a delivery from a spinner which turns from leg to off. An 'off-break' turns from off to leg. That's easy to remember when it's a right-hand bowler bowling to a right-hand batsman. But when a right-arm, off-break bowler bowls to a left-handed bat he is bowling leg-breaks. And a left-hander bowling with an off-break action bowls leg-breaks to a right-hander. It takes some working out- but the drawing helps.

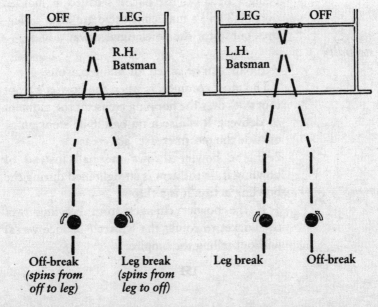

OFF   LEG   LEG   OFF

R.H. Batsman   L.H. Batsman

Off-break *(spins from off to leg)*   Leg break *(spins from leg to off)*   Leg break   Off-break

leg-cutter/ *off-cutter*	A ball which cuts away off the pitch from leg to off is a 'leg-cutter'. The 'off-cutter' goes from off to leg. Both these deliveries are bowled by fast or medium-paced bowlers. See **seam bowling**.
leggie	Slang for a leg-spin bowler.
length	You talk about the 'length' or 'pitch' of a ball bowled. A good length ball is one that makes the batsman unsure whether to play back or forward. A short-of-a-length ball pitches slightly closer to the bowler than a good length. A very short-pitched ball is called a 'long hop'. A 'half-volley' is an over-pitched ball which bounces just in front of the batsman and is easy to drive.
long hop	A ball which pitches very short. See **length**.
maiden over	If a bowler bowls an over without a single run being scored off the bat, it's called a 'maiden over'. It's still a maiden if there are byes or leg-byes but not if the bowler gives away a wide.
no ball	'No ball' can be called for many reasons. 1 The most common is when the bowler's front foot goes over the popping crease at the moment of delivery. It is also a no ball if he steps on or outside the return crease. See **crease**. 2 If the bowler throws the ball instead of bowling it. If the arm is straightened during the bowling action it is a throw. 3 If the bowler changes from bowling over the wicket to round the wicket (or vice versa) without telling the umpire.

4 If there are more than two fielders behind square on the leg side. (There are other fielding regulations with the limited overs game. For instance, the number of players who have to be within the circle.)

A batsman can't be out off a no ball, except run out. A penalty of one run (an experiment of two runs is being tried in county cricket) is added to the score and an extra ball must be bowled in the over. The umpire shouts 'no ball' and signals like this:

over the wicket   If a right-arm bowler delivers the ball from the right of the stumps (as seen by the batsman) ie with his bowling arm closest to the stumps, then he is bowling 'over the wicket'. If he bowls from the other side of the stumps he is bowling 'round the wicket'.

pace   The pace of the ball is the speed it is bowled at. A fast or pace bowler like Waqar Younis can bowl at speeds of up to 90 miles and hour. The different speeds of bowlers range from fast through medium to slow with in-between speeds like fast-medium and medium-fast (fast-medium is the faster).

pitch	See **length**.
reverse swing	Reverse swing occurs when the ball is old and one side of it has become roughed up. Under these conditions some fast bowlers will make the ball swing away from the roughed-up side of the ball. No-one really knows why it happens.
round the wicket	See **over the wicket**
seam	The seam is the sewn, raised ridge which runs round a cricket ball.
seam bowling	Bowling – usually medium to fast – where the ball cuts into or away from the batsman off the seam.
shooter	See **grubber**.
spell	A 'spell' of bowling is the number of overs bowled in succession by a bowler. So if a bowler bowls six overs before being replaced by another bowler, he has bowled a spell of six overs.
swing bowling	A cricket ball can be bowled to swing through the air. It has to be bowled in a particular way to achieve this and one side of the ball must be polished and shiny. Which is why you always see fast bowlers shining the ball. An 'in-swinger' swings into the batsman's legs from the off-side. An 'out-swinger' swings away towards the slips.
trundler	A steady, medium-pace bowler who is not particularly good.
turn	

turned a long way' or 'it spun a long way'.

wicket maiden

An over when no run is scored off the bat and the bowler takes one wicket or more.

wide

If the ball is bowled too far down the leg side or the off-side for the batsman to reach (usually the edge of the return crease is the line umpires look for) it is called a 'wide'. One run is added to the score and an extra ball is bowled in the over.

In limited overs cricket wides are given for balls closer to the stumps - any ball bowled down the leg side risks being called a wide in this sort of 'one-day' cricket.

This is how an umpire signals a wide.

yorker

A ball, usually a fast one - bowled to bounce precisely under the batsman's bat. The most dangerous yorker is fired in fast towards the batsman's legs to hit leg stump.

FIELDING

backing up

A fielder backs up a throw to the wicket-keeper or bowler by making sure it doesn't go for overthrows. So when a throw comes in to the keeper, a fielder is positioned behind him to cover him if he misses it. Not to be confused with a *batsman* backing up.

chance	A catchable ball. So to miss a chance is the same as to drop a catch.
close/deep	Fielders are either placed close to the wicket (near the batsman) or in the deep or 'out-field' (near the boundary).
cow corner	The area between the deep mid-wicket and long-on boundaries where a *cow shot* is hit to.
dolly	An easy catch.
hole-out	A slang expression for a batsman being caught. 'He holed out at mid-on.'
overthrow	If the ball is thrown to the keeper or the bowler's end and is misfielded allowing the batsmen to take extra runs, these are called 'overthrows'.
silly	A fielding position very close to the batsman and in front of the wicket eg silly mid-on.
sledging	Using abusive language and swearing at a batsman to put him off. A slang expression – first used in Australia.
square	Fielders 'square' of the wicket are on a line with the batsman on either side of the wicket. If they are fielding further back from this line, they are 'behind square' or 'backward of square'; if they are fielding in front of the line ie closer to the bowler, they are 'in front of square' or 'forward of square'.
standing up/ standing back	The wicket-keeper 'stands up' to the stumps for slow bowlers. This means he takes his position

immediately behind the stumps. For fast bowlers he stands well back – often several yards for very quick bowlers. He may either stand up or back for medium-pace bowlers.

GENERAL WORDS

colts County Colts teams are selected from the best young cricketers in the county at all ages from Under 11 to Under 17. Junior league cricket is usually run by the County Colts Association.

under 11s/ 12s etc You qualify for an Under 11 team if you are 11 or under on September 1st prior to the cricket season. So if you're 12 but you were 11 on September 1st last year, you can play for the Under 11s.

FIELDING POSITIONS

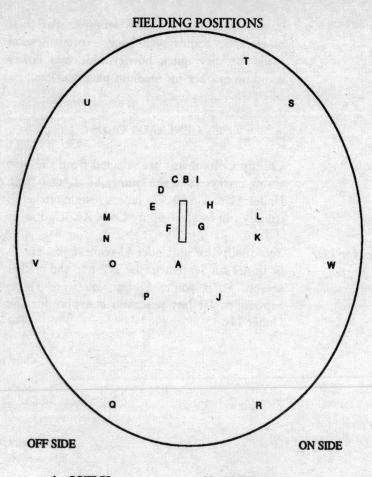

OFF SIDE

ON SIDE

A **BOWLER**	M **POINT**
B **WICKET-KEEPER**	N **COVER POINT**
C **FIRST SLIP**	O **EXTRA-COVER**
D **SECOND SLIP**	P **MID-OFF**
E **GULLY**	Q **LONG-OFF**
F **SILLY MID-OFF**	R **LONG-ON**
G **SILLY MID-ON**	S **LONG-LEG**
H **BACKWARD SHORT LEG**	T **DEEP FINE-LEG**
I **LEG SLIP**	U **THIRD-MAN**
J **MID-ON**	V **DEEP EXTRA COVER**
K **MID-WICKET**	W **DEEP MID-WICKET**
L **SQUARE-LEG**	